Sherlock Holmes and the
Knave of Hearts

Sherlock Holmes and the Knave of Hearts

Steve Hayes & David Whitehead

ROBERT HALE · LONDON

© Steve Hayes and David Whitehead 2013
First published in Great Britain 2013

ISBN 978-0-7198-0794-7

Robert Hale Limited
Clerkenwell House
Clerkenwell Green
London EC1R 0HT

www.halebooks.com

A catalogue record for this book is available from the British Library

2 4 6 8 10 9 7 5 3

Printed in the UK by Berforts Information Press Ltd

'You can file it in our archives, Watson.
Some day the true story may be told.'

– Sherlock Holmes,
The Retired Colourman

This is for our good friend
John Saxon

Prologue

———⌒⌒———

They said he was mad, but of course he wasn't. He was just
… different.

He was bright, studious and conscientious – everyone said
so. But more than that, he was an individual with ideas of his
own. And that's what scared them.

He had never been one to follow the crowd. He was like his
uncle in that respect. That was why they had gravitated
towards each other. They understood each other's needs.

And that was the other problem. Their close affection, along
with his potential brilliance, had inspired jealousy in those
around him – a jealousy that gnawed away at them until eventually they could no longer stand to have him around.

So they sent their poor little Gaston – *regrettably,* they said
– to the alienists, who bombarded him with obscure tests and
questions and then, despite his insightful answers, said simply
what they had been paid to say: that he was suffering from a
'melancholy madness and monomania of persecution' that was
incurable.

With the willing – no, the *eager* – cooperation of his family,
they had locked him away here, in this stately sanatorium in
the heart of the densely wooded Forêt de Russy, far from
prying eyes. They could disown him now; pretend he had never
existed. He would never embarrass them again.

Well, he thought grimly, *we shall see about that.*

Gaston had never slept well, not even when he lived at
home. Here, in this grey stone prison that masqueraded as an

asylum, sleep was practically impossible. At night they came to life, those poor unfortunates who really *were* mad. As darkness fell there came a palpable sense of expectancy that had nothing to do with imagination. Some nights you could actually *taste* it in the air. A grim, heavy silence would drape itself across the building like a shroud. It seemed as if the whole world held its breath and waited.

And then, as the moon rose beyond his barred window, it would begin: the cacophonous symphony of gibbering, screeching, screaming and sobbing. It echoed through the building, mingled with the incessant, hyena-like peals of insane laughter. The rest was a mixture of shouting from inmates like himself, protesting their sanity, trying to make the warders realize there had been a terrible mistake; that they should never have been confined here in the first place; that they were sane – *sane!* – just as he was.

But of course, no one ever listened. They weren't paid to listen. They were paid to pronounce man, woman or child insane and take them off the hands of those who were ashamed of them.

Gaston turned onto his side and pulled the sheet over his head. He shivered. There was no heating here, not even on the bitterest nights. There was no need, they said. Mad people didn't feel the cold, so why waste money keeping them warm?

God, how little they knew – or cared.

Beneath him the springs of his narrow cot squeaked with every move he made. It was a sound he had heard a thousand times before, a sound he normally ignored. But tonight, for some unknown reason, it triggered a reaction in him and suddenly he started sobbing.

The days here were bad enough, but it was so much worse at night. At least during the day they tried to keep the patients occupied. At night, unable to sleep for all the screaming and wailing, Gaston had plenty of time to think, to remember – to plot his revenge.

But even with the sheet over his head he couldn't blot out the noise. Fighting back tears, he lowered the sheet, rolled onto his back and stared up at the shadowy ceiling. He could hear the warders hurrying along the wood-panelled corridors above and below him. He heard the clomp-clomping of their hob-nailed boots on the stone floor, the heavy, echoing slam of their batons against locked doors and their callous, angry threats to whip patients who did not stop yelling. It never worked. Threats fell on deaf ears here. The moaning and weeping would continue until dawn.

Gaston wondered what his family would say if they knew what had become of him. Would they finally understand just how they had condemned him? Or even *care*? The mean little room, barely three metres square, had stolen away whatever dignity he had left. A cot, a chair, a scratched lowboy were his only companions.

Suddenly he stiffened. Heavy footsteps came echoing along the corridor outside. Two men were approaching quickly and with purpose.

Sitting up, he listened intently. In one respect he was fortunate. The inmates on this floor had always been quieter than the rest. He suspected the staff had put all those of a certain class together; people like himself who had been raised well and knew how to behave themselves in company, but who had alienated themselves from their so-called loved ones and now had to pay the price.

The footsteps drew closer. He wondered what anyone was doing here at this late hour. And who were they coming for?

When the footsteps stopped outside his door, he panicked. Why were they bothering him, especially in the dead of night? After an initial period of rebellion, he had learned to keep to himself and cause no trouble. That way the warders left him alone.

As he retreated into the corner – as if that could somehow protect him! – he heard the grinding click of a key turning in

9

the lock. Then the door opened. Two men appeared in the frame, no more than bulky silhouettes against the weak glow of the incandescent mantles that lit the corridors.

'Who's there?' Gaston asked. 'What do you want with me?'

Wordlessly they closed in on him and tried to grab his arms. Panic claimed him. He had heard so many awful stories about insanity and the way the so-called experts pretended to treat it – by letting blood whole litres at a time, by water-shock or purgatives, emetics or the claustrophobic horror of the so-called tranquillizer chair – that he couldn't even *begin* to control his fear. Was that why they were coming to drag him away at this ungodly hour?

Was it?

Was it?

The cold night air was filled with sounds of struggling as they tried to subdue him. Rough hands grasped his throat, choking him. He vaguely heard their muttered curses as they fought to restrain him. He lashed out blindly, punching and kicking at his assailants. He struck one of them. The man staggered away, his flat black coachman's hat falling to the cold tile floor. By the light from the corridor Gaston saw that the man was dressed in a plain black suit – not the uniform of a warder.

He was a *civilian*!

'W-What do you want with me?' Gaston asked.

'Bastard!' growled the man he'd hit. Rubbing his jaw, he made a crude gesture and added: 'Put him to sleep!'

Then he came at Gaston again, faster, more determined, his fists swinging. One blow hit Gaston on the chin. He fell back, hitting his head against the wall. Stunned, he fought to remain conscious. But now the second man brought out a kerchief and a small green-glass bottle. Quickly, efficiently, he doused the handkerchief in a thick, viscous liquid and then clamped it over Gaston's nose and mouth.

'No! No!' His words came out muffled, barely distinct. He

struggled desperately, fighting not to inhale the sickly-sweet chloroform. But his attackers, knowing it was only a matter of time before he had to breathe, kept him pinned down and waited.

Half a minute passed. At last he could hold his breath no longer. He opened his mouth and instinctively tried to gulp in air. Instead he took in a draught of the anaesthetic. His head immediately began to swim and he screamed ... or thought he did. He was suddenly consumed by a sense of unreality, as if he were in a dream where the walls and floor appeared to be melting. Gradually he went limp. The handkerchief was removed. He was dimly aware of being pulled up. He tried to struggle but his body wouldn't respond. Vaguely, he saw the man bending to retrieve his hat; then felt himself being dragged from the room.

The two men half-carried, half-dragged him along the corridor. He felt his bare toes scraping on the tiled floor. The cries of his fellow inmates were louder now, though no clearer; just mindless zoo-like sounds that articulated an awful, inescapable terror.

At the end of the corridor they stopped. Here, the larger of the two men hefted him roughly across one shoulder. In this fashion they descended a creaking wooden staircase to the ground floor. Gaston, arms dangling loosely, saw the steps sliding backwards beneath him. He tried to scream for help, but the chloroform had robbed him of all strength.

On the ground floor he heard someone hiss: '*Quickly!*'

With great effort he turned his head as he was rushed past the speaker towards a rear exit. He knew the man. He was one of the kitchen staff. His name was ... what *was* his name? ... *oui*, Bertrand. Bertrand Joncas. But what was he doing here at this time of night?

'Calm down!' snarled the first man. 'You've earned your money. Your part in this is over now.'

Outside, in the dark bitter night, the man carrying Gaston

crunched purposefully across the gravel drive. Presently he stopped and set Gaston down. Swaying unsteadily, Gaston felt the cold night air numbing his sweated skin. He shivered; tried to hug his thin nightshirt closer to him. Why were they taking him from this place? Had his family had a change of heart? Did they want him back? Or were these men simply moving him from one madhouse to another? Perhaps one that was even worse?

He lost his balance and thought he was going to fall. Instead he slammed against the side of a black coach. He reached out blindly, grabbed a glossy red-spoke wheel and steadied himself. A horse whinnied and stamped its hoofs. Someone draped a coarse blanket over Gaston. Then a new voice inside the carriage said: 'Quickly! Get him inside!'

The voice belonged to a woman.

Gaston frowned. Did he know her? Was it his sister, Marie? The question formed on his lips but he was still sluggish from the chloroform and his tongue felt like a sleeping slug in his mouth.

The two men now manhandled him into the coach and climbed in beside him. He vaguely became aware of the woman's perfume. It smelled of orange blossom, lavender and honeysuckle. Then one of the men rapped against the roof of the coach. A whip cracked and the coach jerked into motion.

The asylum fell behind them, and the coach was soon lost among the great, silent oaks of Forêt du Russy.

CHAPTER ONE

The Answer to the Solution

Sherlock Holmes turned glazed eyes towards his tormentor and said drily: 'It is customary, I believe, to allow the condemned man one last request.'

His companion, John H. Watson M.D., snorted in exasperation. 'Aren't you being just a *little* dramatic, Holmes? Good grief, man, a holiday isn't likely to kill you. Indeed, it is your very death I am hoping to avoid!'

Ignoring him, Holmes closed his eyes and lay still.

His lack of response frustrated Watson. 'I would have expected more gratitude than criticism,' he grumbled. 'But sometimes, Holmes, I swear your gratitude is as hard to come by as your cooperation.'

Again, Holmes neither responded nor moved.

Around them, his room was dim and claustrophobic, the air tainted with a sickly odour that was faintly reminiscent of kerosene. The heavy burgundy curtains were closed and all that could be seen of Holmes himself was an indistinct stick figure almost lost amidst a tangle of sweaty bed sheets.

It pained Watson to see his friend in this sorry condition. Normally fastidious in his toilet, Holmes now lay unwashed and unkempt. Gaunt even at the best of times, he now looked positively skeletal, and somehow much shorter than his normally impressive six feet plus. His grey eyes, usually so incisive, now seemed flat and bloodshot, the oiled black hair that swept back from his high forehead in disarray.

What made it worse was that Holmes's condition was all of his own making.

Brilliant though he was, he was also of sensitive temperament and prone to depression. He lived only to solve the seemingly insoluble, and when there was a scarcity of problems to occupy the cool, analytical machine that was his mind, it was not uncommon for him to fall into a state of deep despair.

At such times Holmes would shut himself away in his spartanly furnished room at their upper Baker Street lodgings and endure the agony of his growing frustration until he could endure it no more. Then, much to Watson's dismay, he would seek solace in a seven per cent solution of cocaine – which explained the sickly, kerosene-like smell that now permeated the air.

The opiate gave Holmes an escape of sorts from the dark thoughts that plagued him. He saw no harm in the practice of injecting it. As a doctor, however, Watson viewed the drug and its after-effects much differently.

It was all well and good for the armies of the world to extol cocaine's ability to lift the mood and reduce fatigue. Even Freud, the Austrian neurologist, had recommended it for the treatment of certain mental and physical conditions, claiming that it brought about a feeling of 'exhilaration and lasting euphoria, which in no way differs from the normal euphoria of the healthy person'.

But as the weeks had passed and still no new or intriguing cases had presented themselves, Watson was forced to watch Holmes's dependence upon the drug grow even as his constitution diminished.

He had lodged with his trusted companion now for more than half a decade, and held tremendous affection for him. Holmes was the finest man he had ever known; one for whom he would willingly lay down his own life. And so it had quickly become impossible for him to stand idly by and watch Holmes slowly but surely kill himself.

Something had to be done to draw him back from the abyss. At first Watson had tried to reason with him. But of course, Holmes had never been a man to reason with. When argument proved similarly futile, Watson was forced to take a tougher stance.

'I am taking you out of London for a few weeks,' he declared, limping unannounced into Holmes's room that chilly March forenoon. 'You have pushed your body to its very limits, and if we are to restore your constitution you need a period of good, clean country air, simple, rustic food and to be among the joys of nature.'

From the sweat-stained bed, Holmes had croaked: 'Leave me be.'

But Watson intended to do no such thing. 'Were I to do that I would be negligent not only to my profession, but also to my dearest friend,' he replied. 'Hear this, Holmes. I will not take no for an answer – your health is far too important. Now, you may pack for yourself or I shall ask Mrs Hudson to do it for you. But make no mistake about it – you *are* taking this holiday.'

Through the poor half-light Holmes gave a thin, disparaging smile. 'However bracing the air may be in Worthing or Eastbourne at this time of year,' he said, 'I fear it will do little to alleviate my condition. I need work, Watson! My brain rebels against stagnation. But where is the challenge? I do not think I shall find it there.'

'We are going farther afield than Eastbourne, Holmes. We are going to *France.*'

Holmes looked aghast. '*France?* What on earth for?'

'Because you have a friend there – a good one – and it will do you good to visit him.'

Holmes's long, chemical-stained fingers gripped at the rumpled sheets. 'You refer, of course, to Henri Gillet?'

'Yes. Gillet. I wrote to him last week and received his reply this very morning. As I expected, he will be delighted to have us.'

Although Watson had taken it upon himself to contact Gillet

about Holmes's condition, he still wasn't entirely sure of the connection between the two men. He knew only that Holmes had performed some unspecified but vital mission for the French government several years earlier, during the course of which he had been called upon to liaise with Gillet, who was then a middle-ranking civil servant working within the *Ministère de la Justice*.

'It's all arranged,' he continued, hoping his enthusiasm would be contagious. 'We will be staying at Gillet's country villa, just outside Amiens.'

'Where I shall be forced to listen to all manner of boring political chit-chat,' complained Holmes.

Ignoring his friend's pessimism, Watson said: 'I've heard that Gillet keeps an excellent cellar, and I'm sure Madame Gillet employs an equally excellent cook. We shall dine well there, I think.'

'I have no appetite at present.'

'The clean country air will soon remedy that. And then, of course, there are the children – Arnaud, Victor and Sophie, I believe. There is nothing quite like a child for helping one put things into their true perspective.'

'I *detest* children.'

'Then you have my sympathy, Holmes, because it is a done deal,' said Watson soberly. 'The *answer* to the *solution,* if you will.' A smile stirred his sandy moustache, for he was pleased with the pun. 'And no amount of argument will change it. Now, clean yourself up, man, or shall I ask Mrs Hudson to give you a sponge bath while I'm at it?'

He started to leave.

'Watson.'

Watson paused and looked back at him. 'Yes?'

'Surely, as a condemned man, I should be allowed one last request.'

'I would hardly consider you a condemned man, Holmes, but … very well, make your request.'

'It is a simple one,' Holmes said weakly. 'There is a man who lives in Amiens, a friend I have long admired. He is one after my own heart, a man of science, intellect, instinct and foresight. I cannot pass through Amiens without introducing myself to him. What's more, I believe he will be altogether more stimulating company than poor Henri Gillet!'

Watson frowned. 'I don't understand. In one breath you call this man a friend, and in the next you imply that you have never even met him.'

'I haven't. And that is why I cannot miss the opportunity now. We have corresponded for years, he and I, albeit irregularly. I am a great admirer of his work, and it pleases me to say that the admiration is mutual. Indeed, I venture to say that you will find him equally fascinating, Watson.'

'Why so?'

'Because he, like you, is a writer,' said Holmes. 'His name is Jules Verne.'

CHAPTER TWO

The Man Who Watched Raindrops

'Jules Verne?' Watson exclaimed. '*The* Jules Verne?'

'I know of no other.'

'By God, Holmes, you never fail to surprise me. I had no idea you knew Jules Verne!'

'We are correspondents,' Holmes repeated. He rose up on one elbow and – to Watson's delight – appeared to warm to the subject. 'As you know, my taste in fiction is usually deplorable. And yet in Verne I have always found the most interesting, challenging and forward-thinking mind at work. His book *Journey to the Centre of the Earth*, for example – and here I refer to the original French text and not the abridged English translation – is an exceptional study. After *Twenty Thousand Leagues Under the Sea* – again, the original version, and not Reverend Mercier's bowdlerized and wholly inaccurate conversion – I resolved to write and tell him so. He favoured me with a reply and we have been swapping news occasionally ever since.'

'Well, clearly I should value the chance to meet such a great man,' said Watson. He had just returned from booking their holiday at Cook's in Ludgate Circus, so their itinerary was all set, but he could see no reason why they shouldn't break their journey at Amiens for a day or so in order to meet Verne. 'Obviously I am delighted to grant your request.'

'Then you had better telegraph ahead and forewarn him,' Holmes advised. 'And also tell Henri we shall be delayed for a time.'

'I shall do so this very minute. Now, stir yourself, Holmes. We leave first thing tomorrow morning.'

His hand was on the doorknob when Holmes again called his name.

'Yes, Holmes?'

A rare smile narrowed Holmes's tight white lips. 'It is as well that someone in this world has my best interests at heart,' he said softly. 'Thank you, old friend.'

After registering their luggage so as to avoid delays in Calais, they caught the boat train from Charing Cross Station early the following day; and as the morning wore on, so London, Lambeth, Lewisham and Bromley gradually yielded to the orchards and woodlands of picturesque Kent.

The day was cool and cheerless. A heavy drizzle fell steadily from the leaden sky. But nothing could dampen Watson's spirits. Holmes's friendship with Jules Verne had come as a very pleasant revelation to him.

Though the prolific author had yet to find true recognition in Britain, he was held in high regard in his native France, where his many exotic fantasies – including *From the Earth to the Moon, The Floating City, Eight Hundred Leagues on the Amazon* and others – had made him a wealthy man. It was going to be a true privilege to meet him.

Holmes, by contrast, was now quiet and withdrawn. Watching him covertly, Watson suspected that his friend was undergoing the effects of opiate withdrawal.

Although his use of cocaine was infrequent, Holmes had taken far more than was wise over the past several weeks. Now, as he stared out of the window at the passing smudge of Kentish countryside, he alternated between restlessness and fatigue, agitation and a generalized malaise.

Suddenly Watson had mixed emotions. He wondered if this holiday had been such a good idea after all. Holmes was clearly not up to it, and as a doctor he should have realized as much.

Then again, Holmes needed distraction at the moment, and that was certainly what this break promised to provide. Watson decided to make no comment and merely monitor Holmes's condition as the days progressed.

The train finally steamed into Dover and they hurried through the rain towards the eastern docks. Here, following a brief wait, they caught the ferry to Calais. Shortly thereafter England's famous white cliffs fell behind them and Holmes shrugged out of his damp double-breasted frock coat and finally began to doze.

The choppy Channel crossing took just under two hours. By the time they set foot on French soil the sea air had sharpened Watson's appetite. Even Holmes seemed somewhat invigorated. They ate a light meal at the Grande Café on the corner of Boulevard Jacquard and Rue Lafayette, then caught the train to Boulogne-sur-Mer, where they would have to change for Paris.

Forty minutes later it was raining even harder as they and their fellow passengers took shelter beneath the platform awning at La Gare de Boulogne-Ville and waited to make their connection. Watson shifted his weight from one foot to the other and cursed the old leg wound that still plagued him in damp weather.

Beside him, Holmes's attention was focused on a young man who stood apart from everyone else. Protected from the downpour by the edge of the awning, he seemed to be staring up into the grey sky with unusual intensity. Holmes watched him for several moments before realizing that the young man was actually watching the rain dripping steadily from the awning's serrated eaves.

'What do you make of that fellow, Watson?' he asked with a subtle wave of his cane.

Watson looked and saw a man in his mid-twenties with a high forehead above dark, brooding eyes and a sober, thin-lipped mouth.

'A school teacher, perhaps?'

Holmes sighed. 'Look again.'

Watson studied the young man more closely. 'Ah-hah,' he said shortly. 'Now I have it, Holmes. He's an amateur meteorologist. See, he has a distinct interest in this dismal weather.'

'I suspect that it is rather more serious than that. In fact, I believe him to be in no small emotional distress.'

'How so?'

'There is something about his expression, a look of fear that is, perhaps, aggravated by no small degree of paranoia.'

Watson's eyebrows arched in surprise. 'And I fear that *you*, Holmes, have been reading too many of Emil Kraepelin's papers. Kraepelin may be the founder of modern scientific psychiatry, but I must remind you that he is also roundly criticized for his wild claims that schizophrenia is a biological illness—'

'—in the absence of any detectable histological or anatomical abnormalities,' concluded Holmes irritably. 'Yes, yes, I am well aware of that. Nevertheless, this young man is distressed. You will note that he has set himself apart from the rest of the passengers. Clearly he wishes to be alone. Furthermore, he holds himself with considerable rigidity, which is suggestive of muscle tension. He displays an unhealthy pallor and his eyes are both bloodshot and ringed with dark shadows. The fact that he is swaying slightly suggests a degree of light-headedness. He is constantly wetting his dry lips, and flexing his fingers nervously. And observe, if you will, the sorry state of his coat and trousers. The poor fellow has neglected his appearance for some time now.'

'So he is not especially interested in the weather?' Watson said, crestfallen.

'On the contrary, he is fixated upon it.'

'And that implies some sort of emotional distress to you?'

'My dear fellow, it is beyond dispute.'

Watson pondered this briefly before saying: 'You are familiar with the concept of Occam's Razor, of course?'

'That one should not increase, beyond what is necessary, the number of entities required to explain anything? Of course.'

'Then may I suggest that the simplest explanation is also probably the most likely? I put it to you that he has set himself apart from the crowd because he is by nature a loner. The flexing fingers could be a subconscious habit of long-standing, or signify anxiety about a forthcoming appointment – which would also explain the constant wetting of his lips. As for the muscle tension, that is most likely because his line of work requires him to sit or adopt an unusual posture for considerable lengths of time.' He chuckled. 'That is the problem with the layman, Holmes, and as a locum I see it on a daily basis. Based upon your observations, you could as easily diagnose that poor fellow with shingles as with a herniated disc.'

'Nevertheless, he is a man with problems,' Holmes muttered darkly.

Watson replied profoundly: 'Show me one who isn't.'

CHAPTER THREE

___❧___

To Absent Friends

Amiens is a picturesque city that lies north of Paris and south-west of Lille. The capital of the Somme departement of Picardy, the metropolis is filled with wide, tree-lined boulevards and narrow canals, impressive Gothic cathedrals and street after street of quaint little shops, each of which appears to lean crookedly against the next. With a population of some 90,000 inhabitants, it was built largely upon the manufacture of textiles – predominantly linen, wool, silk, cashmere and velvet.

The rain had finally stopped by the time their train pulled into Gare du Nord amidst much belching of smoke and blowing of whistles. As they made their way out of the terminus, with its grand brick and glass edifice, Holmes and Watson were just in time to see the clouds to the west break apart and reveal a long-awaited glimpse of blue sky.

But Holmes could only grimace. The station's impressive façade was plastered with posters calling for the resignation of Charles de Freycinet, the country's Opportunist Republican prime minister. 'Now we are *guaranteed* a surfeit of political chit-chat when we see Henri,' he lamented. 'I am afraid I have been so ... distracted ... of late that it quite escaped my notice that France was in the throes of election fever.'

'It isn't,' Watson replied. 'At least not officially. As you know, de Freycinet has only been in power for two months, but apparently there is a feeling here that he has somehow betrayed the people.'

'How so?'

'He was elected upon a whole raft of election pledges, but so far has focused upon only one – the expansion of France's colonies, which, as you know, means little to the man in the street. Even his own party has expressed its disappointment in him.'

'And so the people are calling for him to go.'

'According to *The Times*, he will not last out the year.'

Holmes offered a humourless smile. 'If there is one thing history has taught us, it is that prime ministers do not last long in the Third Republic.'

Watson stopped and listened. 'Is that *fireworks* I can hear?'

Holmes thought a moment before saying: 'Of course! Lent is almost upon us, Watson. The locals must be celebrating it with a carnival.'

'Then it is not *all* doom and gloom,' said Watson, guiding his friend to one side of the entrance. 'Wait here, while I go back inside and make arrangements for our luggage to be taken on to Henri's.'

But Holmes wasn't listening. Again his attention had been taken by the young man who had earlier been so fascinated by the weather. Now the fellow strode past them, breaking step abruptly when he noticed the last of the rain dripping from the entrance overhang. Pausing, he stared up at it for a moment, his mouth slackly agape. Then he pushed aside a political canvasser who tried to hand him a leaflet calling for de Freycinet's removal and marched determinedly along the centre of the facing street, splashing through puddles and shouldering a path between the crowds as if he had no idea they were there.

'Charming fellow,' Watson muttered.

Shaking his head, he limped back into the station to make the necessary arrangements for their luggage. When he saw an attractive woman in a deep purple walking skirt and matching jacket coming towards him from the opposite direction, he moved quickly to open one of the heavy station doors for her.

'*Merci, m'sieur,*' she said, smiling up at him.

Beneath the feathered jockey hat and velvet train that completed her attire, her glistening blue-black hair was brushed to the back of her head, where it was caught up in a cascade of short curls and bound in with a heavy plait. Her face, he thought, was as close to flawless as it was possible to get. She had wide, intelligent green eyes, a short, straight nose, delicate pouty lips and a strong, pointed jaw. She was, he guessed, about thirty.

Touching the tips of his fingers to the brim of his camel-coloured derby, he replied gallantly: 'The pleasure is all mine.'

Her smile broadened, revealing excellent, bone-white teeth. 'English, *m'sieur?*'

'*Oui.*'

'Your French is very good,' she said in careful English.

He beamed at her. 'Why, thank you, *ma'amselle.*'

As he continued on his way, there was a new spring in his step.

By the time he got back to Holmes, the sun was shining but a brisk wind continued to peg the temperature back. Reporting that their luggage would be forwarded to the Gillet residence by the next available train, he added proudly: 'I obtained directions to Verne's house while I was about it. You know, Holmes, my French must be better than I thought. There were no communication problems at all.'

'You always were a man of many talents, old friend,' muttered Holmes.

'Well, according to the baggage clerk, Rue Charles Dubois is only a short walk from here. Are you up to it?'

'I am not an *invalid,* Watson.'

'My dear friend, that is precisely what you *are* at present.'

They set off through crowded streets filled with a carnival atmosphere, and a leisurely ten-minute walk eventually brought them to their destination.

Verne's house sat at the corner of a countrified, tree-lined street that was reached by way of the broad, busy Boulevard Longueville. A narrow, wrought-iron gate was set into a lichen-covered red-brick wall. It opened onto a paved courtyard bounded on two sides by a charming but somewhat irregular two-storey building flanked by the type of short, round tower so beloved of French architects. Neatly tended flowerbeds added colour to the scrupulously clipped lawns.

As they made their way towards a half-glass conservatory hall that was filled with yet more plants and flowers, so as to form a sort of 'winter garden' that reflected its owner's taste for the exotic, Watson glanced around and noted that the left wing of the house was occupied by various out-buildings and stables. It was such an unusual property that it would not have looked out of place in one of Verne's own fantastical stories.

A procession of light stone steps led up to the front doorway, where Watson tugged on the bell. Somewhere inside the great house a dog began to bark. A few moments later a small woman in a high-necked black dress answered the summons, accompanied by a jet-black spaniel that gambolled around her feet with great enthusiasm.

The woman's grey hair was pulled back from her thin, severe, olive-skinned face and tied in a knot at the back of her head. *'Oui, messieurs?'* she asked, looking from one to the other.

Watson cleared his throat, determined to again show off his masterful command of the language. But Holmes beat him to it, speaking with an ease and fluency that quickly deflated Watson. Not that he should have been surprised – Holmes's grandmother *was* of French extraction, after all.

'I am Sherlock Holmes and this is my companion, Dr John Watson. We have come to see M'sieur Verne, if he is home. We did telegraph ahead.'

The woman smiled and nodded. 'Of course. M'sieur Holmes and Docteur Watson. M'sieur Verne told me to expect you. But

I am afraid he is not here at present. He had a prior engagement at the Union Club that he could not postpone at such short notice. He will not be back until five o'clock.' She took a step backwards, adding: 'You will come in and wait?'

'Thank you, *madame*, but we have no wish to impose upon you. We shall come back later.'

'As you wish, *m'sieur*.'

As they retraced their steps to the street, Watson checked his pocket watch. 'Splendid! That gives just enough time to find ourselves a billet for the night and then do a spot of sight-seeing.'

'Right now I would prefer a cup of coffee,' said Holmes ... and for the first time Watson realized that the symptoms of opiate withdrawal were manifesting themselves again. Holmes's thin face was covered in a fine sheen of perspiration and he was shivering noticeably.

'Come,' he said, taking Holmes by the elbow. 'We passed a coffee shop on the way here.'

They returned the way they'd come. Holmes was quiet, his breathing deep and laboured. It was a relief when Watson was finally able to seat his friend at one of the café's pavement tables and gesture for service.

The worst of the attack had passed by the time their coffee arrived. A hint of colour returned to Holmes's hollow cheeks and his hands, when he reached for his cup, seemed somewhat steadier. 'Perhaps you were right to save me from myself after all, old friend,' he managed ruefully.

Watson shrugged. 'It's been a long day,' he replied, trying to make light of it, 'and there is nothing quite like travel for tiring a man out. I suggest we simply rest here until you are fully recovered.'

Holmes raised his cup. 'Then may I propose a toast to our absent friend?'

Watson smiled. 'To Jules Verne,' he said.

CHAPTER FOUR

The Lamb and the Lion

With the beginning of Lent just days away, the carnival was being held in a park across the road. A raucous combination of circus and street party, it was an opportunity for the city's traditional Christians to indulge themselves to the full before beginning their prolonged period of fasting and penitence. It also provided Holmes with a welcome distraction, and before long he announced that he was fit enough to go in search of a hotel for their overnight stay.

They chose the Hotel Couronne on Rue Laurendeau. After booking two single rooms, they made their way slowly back to the carnival.

There was simply no avoiding it. An enormous Ferris wheel threw its slowly turning shadow down across a midway packed solid with shuffling crowds. Here they spotted a clown juggling before a group of small children; there a gathering of young men and women in gaily painted animal masks trying to burst balloons with darts. Others were trying to climb rope ladders in some sort of race, mostly with comical results. And everything was played out to the accompaniment of tinny calliope music, the clink and cheer of people throwing hoops over bottles to win bagged goldfish and the snap and pop of air rifles at the striped shooting gallery tent.

'Try as I might,' Watson said, grimacing as a group of young men passed them in pink pig masks, 'I simply cannot reconcile carnival with religion. The one is so vulgar, the other so dignified.'

28

'And yet the two are entwined,' Holmes reminded him. 'Look to your Latin, Watson. What does the word "carnival" actually mean?'

'Something to do with meat – as in "carnivorous"?'

'Correct. But more precisely it refers to the *removal* of meat from one's diet – in this case, for a period of forty weekdays.'

Before Watson could respond, a small but clearly militant knot of men came shouldering through the crowd, waving banners and placards calling for Prime Minister de Freycinet to be replaced by an Independent Republican candidate named François Fournier. As Holmes and Watson stood aside and allowed them to pass, a second group – comprised mostly of young men out to enjoy themselves – started yelling that the activists were spoiling the fun and should take their nonsense elsewhere.

The leader of the Independent Republicans quickly wheeled around and pinpointed their critics. Harsh words were exchanged, already excitable tempers flared and abruptly the confrontation turned violent.

As a scuffle broke out, the crowd quickly fell back to give them a makeshift arena in which to fight. Both sides hurled themselves at each other. Fierce struggles broke out. One young man went down and was kicked repeatedly by two Independent Republicans. Another staggered away from the mêlée, clutching a bleeding forehead.

Watson was about to lend assistance to the wounded man but Holmes held him back.

'Let me go, Holmes—' Watson protested.

A second later there was a sudden scream. One of the young men who'd been arguing with the protesters fell to his knees, clutching his stomach.

The handle of a knife protruded from between his bloody fingers.

Several women started screaming.

Watson paled. 'Holmes, let me go! I have to—'

'There is little you can do for that poor wretch,' Holmes snapped. 'I know a killing wound when I see one – and so do you.'

As the young man collapsed onto his face and lay still, someone in the Independent Republican group shouted for them to run. They quickly started shoving through the crowd in all directions, casting their placards aside as they went. In the distance a flurry of police whistles could be heard.

One of the protesters, a burly man in a large cloth cap, came running straight towards them. He clearly expected them to make way for him, as everyone else had. But Watson was having none of it. Instead he stood his ground and clenched his fists. This man was an accessory to murder, and Watson wasn't about to stand by and watch him escape.

When he realized that Watson wasn't going to yield to him, the protester swerved at the last moment, intending to go around him. Hurling his cane aside, Watson made a sudden lunge at him. It was a tackle that would have warmed the hearts of his former team-mates at Blackheath Football Club. He wrapped his arms around the fleeing man's chunky waist and his own weight and momentum did the rest. Both men crashed to the muddy ground.

As his cap flew off, the protester swore and tried to push Watson away. But Watson refused to relinquish his prize. He drew back his fist and punched the Frenchman flush on the jaw. The protester's eyes rolled up into his head and he fell back, stunned.

A moment later several dark-clad, kepi-wearing *gendarmes* poured into the area. Intimidated, the crowd became respectfully quiet. They knew the *Gendarmerie Nationale* were free to deal with any public gathering of more than a dozen people in whichever way they felt appropriate.

As one officer knelt to examine the dead man, Watson dragged the groggy protester to his feet and gestured to a nearby police sergeant.

'Over here!'

'What is going on here?' the sergeant demanded, stamping over.

'This man was part of the group responsible for that poor fellow's murder,' Watson explained, breathing hard. 'It's possible he may be able to give you the name of the devil who actually wielded the knife.'

Some nearby onlookers nodded to confirm Watson's story.

'The killer's first name, at least, is Rémy or René,' called Holmes. 'Immediately after the fight one of his companions called to him, but unfortunately I did not catch it clearly enough to tell you which it is.'

Holmes, who had gone to retrieve Watson's cane, now came back and handed it to him. 'The man you are looking for,' he informed the *gendarme*, 'is about five feet four inches – let us say, approximately one point six metres – and some fifty-seven kilos in weight. He has an olive complexion and dark features, short black hair, large brown eyes, a long nose, a heavy brow. He is wearing a well-worn, tan-coloured sack coat, grey twill trousers and elastic-sided brogans, the left heel of which has recently been replaced. You can see that quite clearly by the tracks he left in the muddy ground. He is also missing the tip of his left little finger and has a small beverage stain upon his right sleeve, just above the cuff.'

The sergeant stared at Holmes in amazement. 'H-How do you know all these things, *m'sieur?*'

'I have eyes,' said Holmes. 'I merely *used* them.'

Recovering from his surprise, the sergeant grabbed the protester, roughly turned him around and handcuffed him. '*Merçi, messieurs.* I will, of course, require statements from you both.'

'Naturally.'

As Watson brushed himself off, he muttered: 'Perhaps I should emulate your methods in future, Holmes. It is considerably less strenuous than the alternative.'

'I beg your pardon?'

'Never mind.' Watson looked up, and noticing the expression of admiration on his friend's face said: 'What? What's the matter?'

Holmes gave one of his rare smiles. 'You never fail to amaze me, old friend. One moment you are as meek as a lamb, the next as fearsome as a lion. You truly *are* the most redoubtable of companions.'

It was high praise indeed, coming from Holmes.

Watson flushed, embarrassed. 'Yes, well … that's enough excitement for one afternoon, I think.'

But the excitement, as he was just about to discover, was only just beginning.

CHAPTER FIVE

Murder is Attempted

After giving their statements to the sergeant, they wearily made their way back along Boulevard Longueville. The broad street was filled with the dispersing crowd and revellers from the park and they were bumped and jostled by people hurrying past. They had almost reached their destination – Verne's house on Rue Charles Dubois – when Holmes noticed a stocky man in a long, navy-blue overcoat and peaked cap walking towards them on the other side of the street. 'I believe that is our man,' he said softly.

'Verne?' asked Watson.

'Verne.'

Watson looked more closely at the fellow. In his late fifties, he had a full grey beard, walked with a sailor's rolling gait, and resembled an old sea-dog.

As they watched, the man turned right into Rue Charles Dubois. A second man, one of Verne's neighbours, waved to him from the front of his own property. Verne, head down and clearly deep in thought, offered no acknowledgement.

He reached the wrought-iron gate in the lichen-covered wall and was just about to open it when another man stepped out from behind one of the beech trees that lined the street.

His face was obscured by a white mask with dark, sad eyes and a downturned mouth: the face of tragedy.

In his left hand he held a pistol.

Spotting the weapon, and momentarily wondering if his eyes were deceiving him, Watson exclaimed: 'Good grief!'

Having seen the same thing himself, Holmes was already looking for a break in the busy traffic so he could cross.

Unable to find one, he decided to chance it anyway. He dashed out in front of an oncoming cab, and the trotting horse shied and reared up in its traces. Holmes leapt aside, raced on and narrowly escaped being crushed from the other direction by the wheels of a drayman's wagon filled with heavy barrels.

'Watch where you're going!'

'Look out, you fool!'

As Holmes sprinted onto the opposite pavement, he heard the man in the mask yell: 'Salaud!'

Then the man fired his pistol.

The weapon spat flame and stone chips flew from the cement frame around the gate. Startled, Verne looked around, perhaps wondering if he had mistaken the sound of the shot for a carnival firecracker or the report of an air rifle inside the shooting gallery tent.

The masked man fired again.

This time Verne felt a searing pain in his left leg. Crying out, he fell against the wall and slid slowly to the ground.

As the masked man came closer, Verne shouted: 'Stop him!'

Across the street, his shocked neighbour heard him but fearing for his own life, hesitated to get involved.

Holmes had no such compunction. Without stopping, he hurled himself at the gunman and they both crashed against the wall. As the man's hat flew off, his light brown hair spilled across his mask.

Holmes tore the gun from the would-be assassin's hand, fully expecting him to resist. But he seemed strangely unaware that he had been thrown against a wall, much less that he had just attempted murder. Puzzled, Holmes dragged the man back to his feet and tore the mask from his face.

As he had expected, he found himself looking into the face of the young man they had first seen at Boulogne-sur-Mer – the troubled watcher of raindrops.

Up close, the remnants of a fading bruise could just be seen upon the young man's chin.

Now that the danger had passed, the neighbour regained his courage and came hurrying over to help. Still the would-be assassin just stood there, motionless, a sad, vacant look in his unfocused hazel eyes.

Cursing him, Verne's neighbour got him in an arm-lock and pushed him face-first against the wall. The impact drew blood. Still the young man offered neither resistance nor reaction.

Catching his breath, Holmes turned to Verne. By now Watson had reached the fallen author and was carefully removing his left high boot and sock so that he could examine the wound. The bullet had struck Verne deep in the lower shin, a few inches above the ankle. It was an ugly wound and it was bleeding fiercely.

A crowd had started to gather. As Watson removed his tie and set about fashioning it into a makeshift tourniquet, he caught a distinctive flash of purple off to his left. Glancing that way, he saw the attractive woman who had complimented him on his French at Gare du Nord standing among the curious, chattering passers-by. He nodded at her and then continued tending to his patient.

Behind Holmes and Watson the gate in the wall now opened and a servant rushed out. Drawn by the sound of the shots, he looked at Verne and exclaimed: '*M'sieur!* What has happened?'

'He's been shot,' Watson said. 'Summon an ambulance at once!'

'As for you …' snarled Verne's neighbour, manhandling the vacant-eyed young man, 'I ought to crack your head open!'

'No, Fréson!' cried Verne. 'Do not hurt him!'

The neighbour looked at Verne in surprise. '*What?* But, *m'sieur,* this man just tried to kill you!'

Verne, face as pale as damp parchment, shook his head.

'Leave him be, I say. He meant no such thing. Of that I am certain.'

'How *can* you be certain?' demanded Fréson.

Verne hesitated, then said: 'Because this man is my nephew, Gaston!'

CHAPTER SIX

The Dreamy Mouse

For one fleeting moment there was total, stunned silence. Then the onlookers started chattering again and Holmes, realizing that someone had to take charge, snapped orders to Verne's servant. 'Help your master inside. It is cold out here and there is the threat of more rain. Watson – help him.'

'Of course....'

Watson had been looking for the woman in the purple dress, but she must have left while he was treating Verne. Now he helped the servant gently lift Verne to his feet, and together they assisted him through the gate towards the house.

A dog – the same black spaniel they'd seen earlier – was still barking furiously. A woman in a long brown dress and pearls was standing in the middle of the darkening courtyard. Hands pressed anxiously against her cheeks, she watched as they helped Verne limp towards her.

'Jules?' she called, alarmed. 'Jules! What happened?'

'It is ... nothing, Honorine,' he said weakly. 'Nothing of ... consequence.'

But she knew better. As soon as she saw his leg wound, the dark, intelligent eyes beneath her delicately arched brows widened in horror. 'My God, you're bleeding!'

'He has been shot,' said Watson. 'But do not worry, *madame*, I do not believe the wound to be life-threatening.'

The woman – obviously Verne's wife, Honorine – was about the same age as her husband. She was above average height and of portly stature, her round, clear-skinned face reflecting a kindly nature. She had a long straight nose, a wide, determined mouth, and wore her silver hair in a centre-part, pinned close to her head.

'Dear God,' she said, 'we must get him inside, quickly!'

Holmes watched the exchange, then turned to Verne's neighbour and said: 'I will take charge of this man now.'

'You are welcome to him,' Fréson said, pushing Gaston roughly towards Holmes. 'Should I call for the police?'

'I imagine they have already been summoned.'

Taking Gaston by the arm, Holmes led him through the gate. Gaston was still docile, hardly aware of his surroundings. As if in a daze, he stumbled up the steps on his way into the house. The spaniel rushed up to meet him, happily sniffing around his legs and wagging its tail. Gaston ignored it.

As Holmes led his prisoner into the hallway, a floorboard creaked underfoot. Honorine, who was watching Watson tend to her husband from the sitting-room doorway, heard the noise and turned around.

Recognizing Gaston, she frowned and said angrily: 'You! Did *you* do this?'

Gaston merely tilted his head to one side and stared down at the rug.

'*Gaston!* Answer me!'

Again, Gaston ignored her.

'Madame Verne?' Holmes inquired.

With effort she drew herself up and stifled her obvious anger. '*Oui, m'sieur.*'

'I fear we have not yet been introduced. I am Sherlock Holmes.'

'O-Oh, yes, of course....' Honorine stopped glaring at Gaston and offered Holmes a troubled smile. 'Jules said you were coming. He was most excited about it, in fact.' She again glared at Gaston before adding to Holmes: 'Forgive my rudeness, *m'sieur.* But as you can imagine, all this has come as a dreadful shock. Did you see what happened?'

'Yes.' Over her shoulder Holmes could see into the dark-walled, copper-ceilinged sitting room where Watson was tending to Verne's injured leg. 'Gaston tried to shoot your husband. Do you have any idea why?'

'None,' she replied, her face creased with emotion.

'You are quite sure of that?'

Honorine didn't answer for a moment. Then, 'I am sorry, *m'sieur*,' she apologized. 'My mind is elsewhere at present. Yes, I am quite sure.'

'*Madame*, is there somewhere quiet I can put Gaston until the police arrive?'

Verne's servant appeared at Holmes's elbow. 'Certainly, *m'sieur*. Please come with me.'

He led Holmes along the hallway to a large kitchen at the back of the house. Holmes sat Gaston in a chair at the table and knelt before him. Gaston gave no indication that he knew Holmes was there. Holmes waved a hand before his face. Still he continued to stare blankly ahead. Under the servant's curious gaze, Holmes tilted the young man's face towards the window and looked into his eyes. The pupils dilated normally. He was not under the effects of any drug, then. And yet –

He straightened up again, looked at the servant and said: 'Watch him. I daresay the police will be here shortly.'

'*Oui, m'sieur*.'

He was just about to turn and leave when he realized that Gaston was still looking towards the window. Holmes followed his gaze, but saw only Verne's landscaped gardens beyond the glass, bordered at their furthest edge by a row of gigantic beeches.

Then he realized that Gaston was not looking out the window, but rather at the copper-lined sink immediately below it … and the tap that was slowly dripping water into it.

He looked back at Gaston. Gaston was staring intently at the tap, his lips twitching as if in anticipation as every successive drip formed, grew heavy and finally splashed into the sink. With every drop he appeared to flinch infinitesimally.

'I shall be back,' Holmes told the servant.

In the sitting room Verne was now resting comfortably in a big easy chair, a glass of brandy in one unsteady hand. He was a big, bluff-looking man with a high forehead and curly silver hair. 'M'sieur Holmes,' he said wearily, 'I am so sorry that you had to witness this unfortunate episode.'

'Do not concern yourself unduly,' Holmes said, shaking hands with him. 'I am only glad that we were on hand to make sure the business ended in no worse a manner.' He indicated Watson. 'You have already made the acquaintance of my friend, Dr John Watson, of course?'

'He has been most kind,' said Verne. 'But what of Gaston?'

'He appears to have retreated into a state of near-catatonia.'

Watson rose. 'Perhaps I should take a look at him.'

'If you would.'

After Watson had gone, Holmes asked Verne: 'Do you know why your nephew would wish to shoot you, *m'sieur?*'

Verne fought a battle with emotion that he did not entirely win. *'Non.'*

Sensing the author wasn't being entirely truthful, Holmes said: 'I do not mean to contradict you, M'sieur Verne, but are you absolutely certain of that?'

Again Verne battled his emotions before replying: *'Oui, m'sieur.* Quite.' He paused, sighed heavily and then smiled as if his thoughts pleased him. 'Gaston – my dreamy little mouse, as I always call him – is very dear to me. I love him as my own. Speaking candidly, M'sieur Holmes, his company was always preferable to me than that of my own son. We have travelled extensively together, to your own country, as well as Scotland, Holland, Denmark.... He is a serious boy, studious, but it was his very seriousness that I always admired.

'However, some months ago Gaston suffered a nervous

breakdown and was hospitalized at Blois. I did not even know he had been released.'

'Perhaps he wasn't,' mused Holmes. 'He may have escaped.'

'Either way, it is of no consequence,' Verne said firmly. 'Aside from this injury, no harm has been done. I fear Gaston is suffering far more than I.'

Holmes glanced around the room. It was neat and homely, its walls lined with framed maps that reflected its owner's great passion for geography. 'Still,' he persisted, 'there must have been some reason why he sought to harm you.'

'Please, M'sieur Holmes,' Verne said tiredly. 'I beg you to let the matter go.'

'I know of one,' said Honorine, behind him.

Holmes turned to her. 'Which was...?'

'Gaston wrote to Jules recently, asking for money,' she explained. 'He said he wanted to move to England. Of course, we knew that his father, Jules's brother Paul, would never allow it. So Jules wrote back and refused the request.'

'And that is all?'

'M'sieur Holmes, we appreciate your concern,' Verne said firmly. 'And you have my deepest apologies for any distress this incident may have caused you. But I must ask you to accept this matter for what it is – nothing more than a silly family argument that has been blown out of all proportion.'

Holmes inclined his spare shoulders. 'As you wish, *m'sieur.*'

At last three *gendarmes* arrived. They were accompanied by a short, slim, dark-eyed detective who introduced himself as Inspector Vincent Mathes. Mathes removed his flat-topped derby hat, finger-brushed his naturally curly black hair, tugged at the cuffs of his black frock coat and quickly checked the knot of his burgundy silk tie. Then he nodded gravely to Verne and his wife. He was perhaps thirty, with bushy brows, flared nostrils, thick lips.

'M'sieur Verne,' he said with a click of his heels. 'May I ask what happened here?'

'It was nothing,' the author said uncomfortably. 'Merely a small and insignificant personal matter. I do not intend to press charges.'

'Perhaps not, *m'sieur*. But a gun was discharged on the streets of Amiens. Whether you wish to press charges or not, that is a serious crime. You have the man in custody, I believe?'

'He is being kept under watch,' Holmes said.

Mathes turned to him. 'And you, sir, are...?'

'My name is Sherlock Holmes.'

Mathes stiffened as if he'd been slapped. 'Are you making light of this matter, *m'sieur*?'

'This man *is* Sherlock Holmes, Inspector,' Honorine confirmed hurriedly. 'He and his colleague, Dr Watson, had just come to pay my husband a visit when the shooting occurred.'

Mathes studied Holmes with new interest. 'You witnessed the shooting, *m'sieur*?'

'I did.'

'Then I am indeed fortunate,' said Mathes, offering his hand. 'Your reputation precedes you, sir. I am a great admirer of your methods. Truly, I could wish for no better witness.' He gestured for Holmes to be seated. 'Please, let us hear the matter as you saw it. Then I will arrest the guilty party.'

'Is that really necessary?' asked Verne, his expression wretched.

'I'm afraid it is, yes.'

'Then I beg you, treat him charitably. He recently suffered a breakdown, and is not himself.'

Mathes studied the writer for a long moment before nodding brusquely. 'For you, *m'sieur*.'

'*Merçi.*'

CHAPTER SEVEN

A Change of Plan

A light wagonette ambulance arrived shortly afterwards and Verne was taken to hospital. As Holmes and Watson took their own leave with a promise to return the following day, Watson shook his head in disbelief.

'What a day!' he declared. 'We witnessed the murder of one man and the near-murder of a second! I don't mean to sound callous, Holmes, but I shall be very glad to return to our hotel and the promise of a little peace.'

'Indeed,' Holmes replied distantly. 'But first we have one last errand to perform – we must reclaim our luggage before it is sent on to Henri.'

'I beg your pardon?'

'I believe we shall be staying here rather longer than first thought,' explained Holmes. 'There is far more to this business than meets the eye.'

'Oh, come now—'

'Verne is not telling us the entire truth.'

'That is his prerogative.'

'According to his wife,' Holmes continued, speaking almost to himself, 'Gaston asked Verne for money and Verne refused. Is that a strong enough motive to then try to murder a beloved uncle?'

Watson sighed. Around them the day was drawing to a close and the streets of Amiens were gradually becoming less busy. The sky had turned a deep Prussian blue and as Holmes had predicted, it had started raining again, though just a light drizzle.

'Gaston is clearly not of sound mind,' Watson replied at last. 'Who can tell how such a man's thoughts work?'

'Nevertheless, he came here with a clear purpose, Watson. And where did he get that rather distinctive gun he used? It was, I believe, a Perrin and Delmas pistol of 1859.'

Watson shook his head in admiration. 'You certainly know your weapons, I'll grant you that.'

'I know that *particular* weapon. It was the first successful double-action, centre-fire pistol ever manufactured in Europe. Furthermore, Verne told me that his nephew was confined to a sanatorium in Blois, following a nervous breakdown. So why did we first encounter him on the station at Boulogne-sur-Mer?'

'Perhaps Boulogne-sur-Mer is *near* Blois.'

'It isn't, you know. It is some five hundred kilometres in the opposite direction.'

'I had no idea your knowledge of France was quite so encyclopaedic.'

'It's not,' Holmes said. 'But Verne is a keen geographer, and as you may have observed, the sitting room into which you took him was replete with maps. I merely consulted one of France during our conversation.'

Watson considered the matter briefly before asking: 'Is it not possible that Gaston was released from the sanatorium?'

'It is possible, but unlikely. You saw him earlier. Did he appear in any way cured to you?'

'Well ... no.'

'In any case, the matter is easily answered. We shall send a wire to the sanatorium first thing tomorrow morning, asking after the facts surrounding the young man's release.'

Watson halted abruptly. 'Holmes,' he said, 'need I remind you that one: this is no concern of yours, and two: you are supposed to be here on holiday?'

'Call it natural curiosity if you like,' said Holmes. 'Ascribe it to our sixth sense. But I can feel in my very core that there is more to this matter than meets the eye. And talking of eyes, were I to turn a blind one to this matter then, as you so rightly pointed out yesterday morning, I would be negligent not only to my profession but also to a friend.'

'Holmes—' Watson began, then stopped. He saw something in Holmes's expression that had been missing for far too long – purpose. Although he personally felt that the matter was, as Verne had said, little more than a family squabble that had gotten out of hand, he was willing to indulge Holmes if the investigation of the matter hastened his recovery. 'Very well,' he said. 'Where do we start?'

'First we shall reclaim our luggage, and then we shall return to the Hotel Couronne for a good night's sleep.' Holmes paused and wearily squeezed his brow. 'You are right, old friend. Travel *does* tire a man out. And I have a feeling that we shall need all our wits to deal with this case. This thing, I believe, is going to get worse before it gets better. Possibly *much* worse.'

CHAPTER EIGHT

V.D.C.

Early the following morning they paid their promised visit to Verne, only to be told by Honorine that, while the writer had passed a comfortable night and was expected to be discharged from hospital later in the day, the operation to remove the bullet from his shin had not gone according to plan.

Fighting back tears, she continued: 'I do not profess to understand exactly what went wrong, but it appears that the surgery caused more damage than the bullet itself, which is still embedded in his shin and will now probably remain there for the rest of his life.' She wrung her hands, her voice choked with emotion. 'He will be crippled for the rest of his days. It will be the ruin of him.'

'I think not, *madame*,' said Watson, kindly. 'He is resilient, and by nature looks to the future. I speak from experience when I say that a limp is nothing. It will soon become as natural to him as blinking or breathing. Besides, from what I saw of your husband last night, I believe it will take considerably more than that to slow him down. He is the very personification of durability.'

'It is kind of you to say so,' she said graciously. 'And I appreciate it.'

'Has there been any word of Gaston?' asked Holmes.

Her face clouded. 'I sent a wire to his father, Paul, late last evening, and received a reply within the hour. He said that

46

Gaston had somehow managed to escape from the sanatorium where he was being treated a little less than a week ago.'

'And his father did not see fit to inform you of this at the time?'

'He did not wish to worry us. Besides, he fully expected Gaston to be recaptured within a matter of hours.'

'And yet he was not,' muttered Holmes. 'Forgive me if I appear to speak out of turn, *madame,* but I sensed from your reaction upon seeing him yesterday that you have little love for Gaston.'

She gave a shrug that was typically French. 'He had just shot my husband, *m'sieur.'*

'You were certainly not pleased to see him before you knew that for a fact.'

'Let us just say that he is not an easy person to like. Too serious. Too … intense.'

Holmes nodded his understanding, but a glint in his grey eyes suggested that he believed there was more to it than that. 'Thank you, *madame.* Perhaps we could call again later today?'

'Please do,' Honorine said. 'It will do Jules good to have visitors. This matter has quite understandably left him shaken.'

'I have just one favour to ask before we leave,' Holmes added as Watson picked up his hat and cane. 'Would you be so kind as to provide me with a letter of authority so that I may speak with Gaston?'

Her face darkened again. 'Why must you do that, *m'sieur?'*

'As you know, crime and its motives are my stock-in-trade, if you will. I hope that I might be able to learn something of both from Gaston.'

'And *I* beg you to leave the matter be, *m'sieur,* if only as a favour to Jules. There has, I fear, been an unhappy history between them. Best to let it lie.'

'As you wish,' Holmes replied. 'Please forgive me for asking.'

Outside, Watson said: 'Well, that rather scuppers your investigation, doesn't it? The police won't allow you to see Gaston without the necessary permission.'

Holmes shrugged vaguely, his mind elsewhere. 'No matter,' he replied after a moment. 'There are more ways than one to skin a rabbit, old friend.'

The stooped, bookish old man with the cracked leather writing-case folio tucked under one arm turned onto the Rue de la Republique and stopped briefly at a corner flower stall. After some deliberation he plucked a single blood-red rose from a vase of water and deftly slid the stem into his button-hole. He then paid for his purchase, nodded his thanks to the vendor and hurried on his way.

He was a fussy-looking man in his sixties, with dusty grey hair, a heavy moustache and a pair of gold-rimmed pince-nez hanging from a ribbon around his neck. He wore a double-breasted frock coat, a grey shawl waistcoat, black trousers that were baggy and stretched at the knees and two-colour, button-up ankle boots.

When he arrived at the central police station all was quiet and Sergeant Gabriel Bessette, who was manning the reception desk at the time, was trying to catch up on some long-overdue paperwork. The bookish, hunched-over man went directly to the desk and rapped his knuckles sharply against the scratched counter to get Bessette's attention.

Bessette looked up, irritated at being disturbed. He was a brawny forty-year-old with a hard, humourless face and thinning brown hair that was already losing its colour. There was nothing of welcome in his manner when he snapped: '*Oui?*'

'Excuse me,' said the newcomer, his voice a high-pitched crackle. 'I am here to see Gaston Verne.'

Bessette scowled. 'And who are you?'

'I am Lucien Menard, of Desmarais, Brun et Chevalier. We have been appointed legal representatives to M'sieur Verne.'

'Upon whose authority?'

'Upon the authority of the accused's uncle, M'sieur Jules Verne.'

'You have papers to this effect?'

'We have only just received his instructions, *Sergent*. The necessary papers are presently being drawn up. I have been sent to take preliminary details of the case.'

Bessette studied the lawyer's clerk a moment, then growled: 'Come back later, when you have the necessary authorization.'

Menard's rheumy eyes widened. 'Do you know what you are asking of me?' he demanded, indignantly fixing the pince-nez to the bridge of his nose. 'Do you know how long it has taken me to walk all the way here from Rue de Mercey? And me with my rheumatism?'

Bessette raised his hands, showing Menard palms that were curiously red. 'All right, all right, keep the noise down.'

'*Non,*' said Menard with a fervent shake of the head. 'Do you know who Jules Verne *is*? He will not take kindly to your obstructive attitude, *Sergent*. Let me see the officer in charge of the case! Perhaps he will take a different view!'

'No need for that,' Bessette said. He considered for another moment, then looked over his shoulder and called: 'Trudel! Take this man down to see Verne – not that he'll get much out of him.'

The *gendarme* nodded and led the lawyer's clerk down a short flight of cold stone steps to a basement area. From there they hurried along a narrow, ill-lit corridor between two rows of sturdy strap-iron doors, into each of which was set a small, covered eye-hole. They stopped before one particular door and the *gendarme* gestured that Menard should submit to a search. The clerk cooperated fully.

When the constable was finished, he unlocked the door, opened it and said: 'Visitor for you, Verne.'

As the door closed behind him, Menard looked around the small cell. The only light came through a narrow barred window at the very top of the wall, which was at pavement level when seen from outside. Gaston sat on the edge of his small mattress, hands clasped loosely in his lap. He looked thoroughly preoccupied with other matters, and unmistakably fearful.

The lawyer studied him for a few moments. Then, after glancing once over his shoulder to make sure they were not being watched through the eye-hole, he underwent a curious transformation. He straightened from his bookish hunch until he stood much taller than he had outside. And when he spoke now, his voice was stronger, more authoritative – the voice of Sherlock Holmes.

'Gaston?' he said softly.

No reaction.

'Listen to me, Gaston.' Holmes set his folio down and dropped to one knee before the young man. 'You are in serious trouble. Very serious trouble. And I am here to help you.'

Gaston didn't answer; didn't even seem aware of his presence.

Slowly, deliberately, Holmes removed the rose from the buttonhole in his lapel. Gaston looked at the flower, watching it with the slightest frown.

Holmes held the rose up in front of Gaston's face. Then he placed the forefinger and thumb of his free hand around its neck. Carefully, he slid his fingers down the length of the stem, avoiding the thorns and squeezing gently as he went. The water the rose had previously absorbed in the vase at the flower stall now gathered at the end of the stalk, and under Holmes's gentle pressure began to drip to the floor.

The effect it had on Gaston was dramatic. His eyes grew large and fearful. He swallowed hard and shook his head several times. Then he backed up against the wall as if to get away from it, and tucked his legs up in front of him.

'Non ...' he whispered. 'Pas à nouveau!'

Holmes held the blood-red rose closer to him. The movement dislodged another drop of water. Gaston's eyes saucered and he flattened fearfully against the wall.

As Gaston watched in undisguised horror, Holmes slowly crushed the flower in one hand and then threw it into the corner of the dismal cell.

'There,' he said. 'It's gone.'

But Gaston's reaction had told him all he needed to know. It also confirmed his suspicion that there was more to all this than had first appeared.

'I want you to think of me as your friend,' Holmes said quietly. 'I'm going to ask you some questions. Answer them truthfully and I will do everything in my power to help you.' Holmes paused to let his words sink in, then said: 'Why are you so frightened by dripping water?'

Gaston opened his mouth, but seemed unable to form words. The best he could manage was a nervous shake of the head.

'It's all right, Gaston. I am here to *help*. I know you were coerced into shooting your uncle. What I need to know now is who coerced you? And why?'

Gaston tucked his chin into his chest and looked up at Holmes from beneath incredibly sad brows. His lower lip trembled. He started to rock back and forth, clearly agitated.

'Who hit you?' Holmes asked, gesturing to the all-but-faded bruise on Gaston's jaw.

Gaston shook his head.

'You will be punished for what you did,' Holmes told him. 'But unless you help me, whoever made you do it in the first place, they will walk free. That hardly seems fair.'

Gaston turned away from him, huddled into a protective ball and continued rocking.

'What did they do to you, Gaston? Whatever it was, I promise they shall never harm you again.'

More rocking.

'Who *are* they, Gaston?'

Gaston turned to face him again. The sadness in his eyes was almost depthless. He leaned forward, again seemed about to speak, then shook his head and hugged himself tighter.

Holmes considered briefly; then, on impulse, took out a scrap of paper and a pencil. He offered them to Gaston. 'Give me their names, and I will see that they are brought to book for this.'

Gaston stared at him for a long moment. In his expression was a mixture of confusion and helplessness. Then, as if reaching a decision, he reached out one trembling hand and took the scrap of paper and pencil. Holmes stood back, waiting. Verne's nephew sat a little straighter and rested the paper on one knee. He started crying as he scrawled:

V D C

'What does this mean?' asked Holmes, taking the paper when Gaston offered it back to him. 'What do these letters stand for?'

But Gaston's only response now was to shake his head and start sobbing. Holmes reached for him, intending to place a comforting hand on his shoulder. But the younger man flinched away from him. Holmes withdrew his hand and nodded to show he understood. 'It's all right,' he assured. 'I know you're afraid of me. But if I'm to help you, Gaston, you *must* trust me.'

Gaston only curled back into a foetal ball.

With nothing more to be had from the man, Holmes once again allowed his shoulders to drop, hunched his back so that he appeared shorter, and knocked on the cell door. 'You may let me out now,' he called in Lucien Menard's high voice. 'I am finished here for the time being.'

CHAPTER NINE

꞉ꞈ

A Waiting Game

Later, back in his room at the Hotel Couronne, Holmes began removing his disguise. 'I am more convinced than ever that this is no mere family squabble,' he told Watson. 'Indeed, I am afraid that Verne may be dealing with an enemy who has considerable resources and no small degree of sophistication.'

Watson was watching him from a chair on the other side of the room. Not for the first time he was amazed by Holmes's ability to alter his appearance. Clothes, hair, posture, speech ... everything would change. He would not simply pretend to be someone else, he would *become* that person. And he would skilfully apply stage makeup from the small kit he rarely travelled without until the illusion was complete.

'What makes you say that?' he asked as Holmes now used a sponge to remove the sallow colour of 'Lucien Menard's' skin.

'You have met Gaston. Do you for one moment believe that he could escape from a lunatic asylum, much less obtain a gun, travel five hundred kilometres to Boulogne-sur-Mer, then vanish or avoid detection for one entire week before coming here with the specific purpose of killing his uncle? No, my friend, he had help every step of the way – and that takes considerable resources.'

'And the sophistication?'

'Have you ever heard of Hippolytus de Marsiliis?'

'I cannot say that I have.'

53

'He was a fifteenth-century lawyer who invented a method of torture by which drops of water are allowed to fall upon the victim's forehead at irregular intervals and thus drive that person insane. After sufficient exposure to such treatment, the victim would be only too happy to reveal his secret, confess to a crime, or indeed agree to do anything his or her captors requested of him.'

'I have certainly heard of water torture, but—' Watson stopped. 'Are you saying that Gaston has been subjected to such treatment? Holmes, this is monstrous! By whom?'

'Let us first consider for what purpose.'

'You mean it wasn't just to drive the poor fellow mad?'

'Watson, Gaston Verne is already hopelessly insane. But his fascination with dripping water, his very real fear of it, tells me that he has been subjected to the treatment for an altogether *different* purpose – to focus his otherwise disordered mind upon one single objective, to kill the man he has been convinced is responsible for all his woes.'

'But why Jules Verne? The man is not only his uncle but a writer, beloved by millions!'

'That is the very thing we have to find out.'

'Again, I say – who did this dreadful thing?'

'This is our only clue,' said Holmes, offering up the scrap of paper.

Watson looked at it. '"VDC"? What does that mean?'

'I do not know, yet – and it was all Gaston could do to *write* it, much less *explain* it.'

'Then what do you suggest we do?'

'The only thing we can do at present, Watson. Wait for them to make their next move, whoever they are … and be ready for them when they do.'

At lunchtime Sergeant Bessette left his post and hurried through the city until he reached Hautoie Park. Given the choice, he would sooner have made a detour to his favourite café first and fortified himself with a cognac. But that would have to wait.

It was a pleasant day and the park was crowded. He strode purposefully through an avenue of plane trees, followed a gravel path past a line of poplars and at last reached a row of benches that overlooked the sizeable, wind-rippled lake that was shaded from the sun by a row of spreading Cypresses. He paused briefly, then casually approached a bench upon which sat an attractive woman. About thirty, she was dressed in a distinctive purple walking skirt and matching jacket.

'May I?' he asked.

She nodded, and he sat down.

'Mademoiselle Denier?' he said.

'I am Lydie Denier, yes,' she replied, continuing to watch the lake. 'What is the problem, Sergeant?'

'I'm not sure there *is* one, yet. But a man came to the station this morning, some crotchety old lawyer's clerk engaged by Jules Verne to defend his nephew against all charges. He asked to speak with him.'

'And you let him?' Lydie asked, still gazing at the lake.

'I could hardly refuse without blowing the matter out of all proportion.'

She considered that for a few moments. Finally she said: 'Do not worry. I doubt he would have learned anything of use from Gaston. The man is now little more than a shell.'

There seemed to be a hint of regret in her tone. But Bessette, wrapped up in his own thoughts, missed it.

'There's more,' he said.

Turning from the lake, she looked at him. 'Go on,' she said tightly.

'Another man arrived two hours later. He too claimed to have been engaged by Verne, to represent Gaston.'

She frowned. 'An imposter?'

'*Non,*' he replied. 'I know this man. I've seen him at more

55

court appearances than I can count. His name is Depaul. He's genuine.'

'Then who was the first man you allowed to see Gaston?'

'He gave his name as Lucien Menard. I made some enquiries. No one has ever heard of him.'

'Then who is he?'

Bessette looked almost sick. 'I think I know,' he confessed uncomfortably. 'You were there just after Verne was shot. Did you notice the two men who immediately came to his aid?'

'*Oui.* I spoke to one of them at Gare du Nord, when we arrived yesterday afternoon.'

'You have heard of Sherlock Holmes, of course?'

'Of course.'

'He was one of them. The other was a man called Watson. His companion, I believe.'

'Are you *sure*?'

'I checked the witness statements.' He paused, then said: 'Do you think Verne has engaged this man Holmes to investigate the matter?'

'I cannot think why. We have been careful to observe complete secrecy throughout. He would have had no call to engage a detective. As far as he is concerned, the matter is cut and dried. But I have to confess, I do not care for this man Holmes's interference.'

Suddenly she turned a little. She was now facing Bessette directly, the anger in her eyes making him flinch. 'You fool!' she hissed. 'You have been uncommonly stupid.'

'How was I to know –?'

'Absalon expects us to know *everything*,' she reminded him. It was true.

'I can take care of it,' he said timidly.

'You will do nothing,' she snapped. 'Do you understand me? You will do nothing until I have referred the matter to a higher authority. Sherlock Holmes is known throughout Europe. To attack him will only draw attention to us – attention we can certainly do *without*.'

'But what about Gaston? May I assume he has outlived his purpose?'

'Assume nothing!' she said, rising. 'Just await my orders.'

'Very well.'

'I will contact you by the usual means, and under the usual alias, when I know more – probably before the end of today.'

'I'll be waiting,' he promised. He watched as she walked away. He now needed a drink more than ever.

CHAPTER TEN

A Bodyguard for Verne

When Honorine ushered Holmes and Watson into the sitting room that same afternoon, they found her husband resting on a chaise longue in the bay window with his bandaged left leg resting on a stool. 'You will forgive me if I do not rise,' he said, weakly extending his right hand.

They shook hands with him and then, at Verne's urging, took seats.

'How are you feeling, sir?' Watson asked.

'I am alive. What more can I ask for?'

'And Gaston? Have you heard how he is?'

'We have sent Jules's lawyer to represent him,' put in Honorine. 'Our hope is that he can convince Inspector Mathes that what happened was merely a silly misunderstanding, and allow him to be returned to the Sanatorium de Russy.'

Holmes narrowed his eyes. 'When did you dispatch your lawyer?'

'I believe he went down to the police station shortly before lunch.'

Holmes and Watson exchanged a look.

'Forgive me, gentlemen, but is something wrong?'

'M'sieur Verne,' said Holmes. 'For reasons I do not yet understand, I believe your life to be in danger.'

'Mine?' Verne gave a short, mirthless laugh. 'I have the greatest respect for your talents, as you know, but I cannot see why that would possibly be.'

'Nevertheless, I should be grateful if you would exercise the greatest caution until the matter is resolved.'

'What matter?'

'That, I cannot say. But I have strong reason to believe that Gaston was acting under duress when he made his attempt upon you yesterday.' He paused, allowing his words to sink in, then stared questioningly at Verne. 'Can you think why that should be?'

'*Non.*'

'Is there anyone, man or woman, you know who might be driven to such lengths?'

'*Non.* I have always tried to keep my business affairs as cordial as possible. You may ask anyone.'

'Do the initials "V.D.C." mean anything to you?'

Verne ran them through his mind briefly and then shook his head.

'Then all I can ask is that you indulge me, and take extra care,' said Holmes. 'You *do* have enemies, M'sieur Verne, and I am convinced that they will make another attempt upon your life. You must be on your guard.'

'And you, my dear friend,' countered Verne, 'must understand that, without a scrap of evidence to support your claim, I cannot take such a threat seriously.'

'I am sorry to hear that. But it is in pursuit of evidence that I must shortly take my leave. In the meantime, I should be grateful if you would allow Dr Watson here to stay on as your guest.'

Verne and his wife exchanged a puzzled glance.

'I do not wish to overestimate the threat, M'sieur Verne,' Holmes continued, 'but you will be considerably safer with Watson by your side. He is as fearless as any man I have ever known, and by far the most reliable.'

'Then if it sets your mind at rest,' Verne said graciously, 'I should be very glad of his company.'

CHAPTER ELEVEN

Absalon

A polished black coach was waiting for Lydie Denier when her train steamed into Paris. The driver opened the door for her and she climbed inside with neither a word nor a glance in his direction. She sat back in the upholstered seat and again found herself wondering what Absalon was going to say when he heard the news. He was not a man to lose his temper. He was too well bred for that. But he *was* a man who despised failure and complication, and here she was, coming to report both.

As Paris fell behind them and she watched the emerald countryside rush past in a blur, she wondered how many times she had been to the magnificent but isolated chateau fifty kilometres to the east. Since Absalon had recruited her twelve months earlier, perhaps eight in all. And yet the prospect of having to come back again, for any reason, never failed to make her uneasy. And more than once during the two-hour train ride from Amiens she had found herself questioning the wisdom of accepting Absalon's invitation to join the organization in the first place.

Not that she had been given any real choice in the matter. She had no idea that he – they – had been watching her for as long as they had. She still had no idea how she had first come to their attention. She had always been careful, or so she thought. And yet they had eventually made their move.

She had been renting a comfortable *appartement* in Lyon at the time, and life had been good – though never quite good enough for Lydie, of course. One afternoon there was a discreet rapping at her door, and when she answered it, the man who called himself Alexandre Absalon had entered her life.

He was a tall, spare man of about fifty. His prematurely snow-white hair swept back from a high forehead in a sharp widow's peak. His eyebrows were thin, grey, his penetrating hazel eyes set deep in their sockets. His nose was long and straight, his mouth wide, almost lipless. His neatly trimmed fork beard gave him an unsettling Mephistophelian aspect.

'Mademoiselle Denier?' he had asked.

'*Oui*. And you are...?'

'Alexandre Absalon.'

The name, then, had meant nothing to her.

Without waiting to be asked, he had brushed past her and into her *appartement*.

She should have tried to bar his way, or demand that he turn round and wait until he was invited inside, but instead she did nothing. His bearing and appearance spoke of wealth, and if there was one thing Lydie prized above all else, it was money. So all she did was close the door behind him and wait expectantly for him to explain his presence.

He took his time about it. He chose the most comfortable chair in the room and sank gracefully into it, then very deliberately removed his exquisite hand-cut and -sewn leather gloves finger by finger. Once he had laid them on the arm of the chair, he tugged fastidiously at the crease in his brown-striped cotton twill trousers.

'I represent an organization that can promise you money and power, in almost unlimited quantities,' he said. 'And we know from our enquiries that you possess a nearly insatiable appetite for both.'

She had made a token protest of innocence, of course. 'I'm sorry, *m'sieur,* but I don't know what you are talking about.'

'Oh, come,' he said. He had a gentle, reassuring voice that was entirely at odds with the hard, unreasonable taskmaster he eventually proved to be. 'We are both busy people. Let us waste no more of each other's valuable time than we need to. We know all about you, Mademoiselle Denier. Or should I call you Adele Veillon, or Josette Corbeil, or Suzanne Morace?'

Although Lydie tried not to betray anything, she knew her expression gave her away. She had no idea that any of her many aliases were known to anyone other than herself.

'You are a con artist,' Absalon said bluntly. 'A very good one. You have worked your tricks from Brest to Monaco and just about everywhere between the two, with enviable success. I might say that you are the best in your chosen profession – and that is what we require, *mademoiselle;* the very best.'

'To do what, *m'sieur?*'

He gestured vaguely with one soft, manicured hand. 'To arrange. To manipulate. To coerce. To guide. To listen and report back. To act as a go-between or a spy. To blend in or be noticed, as the task requires. And if you serve us well, you will be amply rewarded.'

'And if I reject your offer?'

Absalon sighed. 'Then we should be forced – most regrettably – to release the dossier we have compiled upon you and your activities to the *Gendarmerie Nationale,* with the insistence that they hunt you down and arrest you with the utmost dispatch.' He paused momentarily to give her a chance to think about it, then said: 'We can do it, too. We are more powerful than you will ever understand.'

There it was, then. Lydie had no choice but to accept. And yet, was that so bad? Absalon was right. Because she had been born into poverty she had very early on acquired an all-consuming desire for the finer things in life. She had watched her father die when she was six, her mother when she was eight. Both had died from an endless struggle to do the one thing that should have been so easy – simply, to *live.*

Oui, she had seen the poverty in which they had lived and expected her to live, and she had despised it and decided that she would never go cold, or hungry, or barefoot, ever again. From the time she was fourteen, she had decided that. And she had made good upon that promise.

At first she had started with the so-called 'badger game' – using her looks to compel prominent married men to take her to bed, only to later claim to have become pregnant and threaten to tell all if they didn't provide for her and the baby … the baby, of course, who never existed.

Over time she had graduated to the lonely hearts columns, contacting wealthy, lovelorn men by letter, telling them everything they wanted to hear and then agreeing to meet them … if only they could first send her some money to pay for her travel and perhaps some new clothes so she would look her best for them.

It had never failed to surprise her just how many men fell for it. Equally surprising was how many paid up in the expectation that she would actually go through with it and meet, then marry, them.

She next turned to fraud. The money was especially good during that period. But so were the chances of arrest and incarceration. So she took up a different type of con – befriending lonely, elderly widowers, gradually gaining their trust and then coaxing them into spending their money on her. Of all her cons, this was her least favourite. She could override her conscience when it came to conniving money from wealthy professionals or businessmen, but emotional robbery was something else; and troubled by their grief, she soon realized she could not justify her actions or ignore her conscience any longer, and started searching for other ways to con money from the rich.

Lydie had always been careful – or so she'd thought. But somewhere along the way she had come to the attention of this man Absalon and his mysterious employers.

Common sense told her that she should call his bluff, simply say no and then do as she had done so many times before – vanish overnight, set up somewhere new, as *someone* new.

But he had promised money and power. And the way he had promised them told her that he knew well that these were as necessary to her as food and drink, something she needed for her very survival.

'Very well,' she said at length. 'I accept your proposition. When do I start work?'

He smiled, and the smile, like the forked beard, was devilish. 'We will be in touch.'

And a month later they were.

The jobs consisted of travelling around the country under a variety of aliases, showing interest in the workings of local politics, getting to know the public and private sides of various officials and councillors, and reporting back to Absalon. She had no idea why she carried out most of her duties, and knew better than to ask. Absalon would never come right out and tell her. But she was happy with that. Absalon scared her. The nameless organization for which he worked scared her. The less she knew, the safer she felt she would be.

So she resigned herself to being a good little foot soldier in Absalon's army – and it *was* an *army*. Whoever he was, whomever he worked for, Absalon had minions everywhere, digging, bribing, listening, reporting back. And at the centre of his web yet more minions collated and deciphered and interpreted that information.

To what end? She had no idea. At least, not at first. But inevitably her curiosity grew and she began to wonder.

Eventually it was the very name of the organization that gave her the answer. And then she understood what Absalon had meant about almost limitless power.

At last the coach slowed enough to tell her they were nearing the end of the journey. She composed herself as best she could. It would do her no good to let them see just how much this stone-and-slate chateau tucked away at the heart of the Forêt Domaniale de Malvoisine intimidated her. She had to present confidence, dedication to the cause … whatever the cause might be.

The coach followed one of the two gravel drives through a mixture of formal lawns and Italianate terraces. Though it had fallen into decay following the Revolution of 1848, the chateau had been rebuilt during the reign of Napoleon III and now stood in magnificence at the centre of seventeen hectares of land. It had its own lake, a guesthouse and numerous outbuildings, and was hidden away behind a protective enclosure of box and yew trees.

A few moments later the coach pulled up before the wide stone steps that led to the house. One of Absalon's other agents, alerted to her arrival by the telegram she had sent from Amiens immediately following her meeting with Bessette, was waiting to meet her in the cathedral-like reception area, with its cold flagstone floor and central cantilever staircase.

This was Lacombe; she had never discovered his first name and had no particular desire to do so. He was a short, portly man in his mid-forties with a jowly face, a constant shadow to his soft jaw and unruly iron-grey hair that always seemed to be in need of a trim. He was devoted to Absalon, or at least gave that impression. And he had never bothered to disguise the lust she saw in his grey-blue eyes every time he looked at her.

'You're late,' he said. His voice was soft and breathless, the voice of a man who could be almost unimaginably dangerous.

'I am right on time,' Lydie replied.

He shrugged and led her into the spacious downstairs family room that Absalon had converted into his office.

The room was a picture of elegance. Ornate mirrors in solid-gold frames hung beside fifteenth-century paintings on the flawless buttermilk walls. Thick burgundy drapes gathered at each of the windows and clustered in fashionable spills on the patterned carpet. Fine furniture was scattered everywhere –

satin-topped benches, chaise longues, armchairs with velvet cushions and rattan-backed chairs. Two crystal chandeliers sparkled in the weak sunlight.

Absalon was down on one knee before a large brown-and-black Chubb safe, sorting through some papers. The safe, she saw, was filled with files, folders and chunky box folders.

He heard them enter, then quickly rose to his full height and hurriedly closed the safe's two doors before spinning the combination dial. It was the first time she had ever seen him taken by surprise, and she realized with just a hint of satisfaction that he was human, after all.

And also that the safe must contain material of particular importance to him.

After Lacombe had left, Absalon said, 'There has been trouble,' knowing she would not have come otherwise.

Lydie nodded. 'Gaston did as he was instructed, but Verne was only wounded.'

'I know that. The newspapers are full of it. But there is more, isn't there?'

'*Oui*. There were witnesses to the shooting.'

'We expected as much.'

'Of course. But we did not expect Sherlock Holmes and his companion, John Watson, to be among them.'

Absalon was silent for what seemed like a very long time. He stood so still, and for so long, that she fancied that he might suddenly have turned to stone.

At length he said: 'Ah.'

Lydie hesitated before saying: 'Sergeant Bessette told me that a man purporting to be a lawyer's clerk working for Verne visited Gaston this morning. He proved to be no such thing, and upon checking, Bessette discovered that there is no such man.'

'Did this "lawyer's clerk" see Gaston?'

'Yes. But it's doubtful he got anything out of him.'

'Still …' began Absalon. He fell silent again.

Lydie, knowing he wasn't finished, didn't say anything.

Presently he said matter-of-factly: 'Have Gaston killed. He is of no further use to us.'

It was all she could do not to flinch at the utterly callous way he'd given the order. 'And Holmes?' she asked.

'Find out what he is doing in France, whether or not there is any connection between him and Verne. It could just be coincidence.'

His tone said that he doubted it.

'And Verne?' she asked.

'According to the papers, he was wounded in the leg.'

'Yes. The wound is not life-threatening.'

'No. And yet, if blood poisoning were to set in....'

'Do you want me to arrange it?'

'Not yet. We'll give Verne another few days. He has no reason to suspect the real reason he was targeted. Hence, he cannot tell Sherlock Holmes anything he doesn't know. But eventually he may become more ... cautious.' He fixed her with a steely glare, his plans made. 'Get close to him. Find out what he thinks or suspects – if anything. And then arrange for that unfortunate case of blood poisoning.'

'Is that all?'

Absalon nodded.

'So for now it is just ... Gaston?'

'Just Gaston. Oh, and Lydie?'

'Yes, M'sieur Absalon?'

'Tell Bessette there must be no more mistakes. I do not take kindly to disappointment, and neither do the men for whom we both work.'

'Trust me,' she said. 'There won't be.'

CHAPTER TWELVE

Of Titles and Plots

As night fell over Amiens, Jules Verne stroked the head of his black spaniel, Follet, then looked at his guest and said: 'I began to write at the age of twelve. It was all poetry then, and quite dreadful poetry, too. But even then I remember spending a long time over my writings, copying and correcting, and never really feeling satisfied with what I had done. And that method of work has clung to me throughout my life. In all modesty I may say that I don't believe I have ever done a slovenly piece of work.'

It was a little after seven o'clock, and they had dined well on spinach salad and beef short ribs braised in Cabernet, served with pasta, pearl onions and mushrooms. They had topped the meal with toasted *pain d'épices*, a mouth-watering mixture of gingerbread and hazelnuts that Madame Verne herself had prepared in honour of their guest.

Afterwards, the two men – Verne swinging himself along awkwardly between a pair of crutches supplied by the hospital – withdrew to a small lounge Verne referred to as 'the smoking room'. Here they settled into comfortable chairs either side of a large Regency fireplace, each to enjoy one of Verne's excellent Havana cigarros.

'I am surprised to hear you talk of poetry, sir,' said Watson, who had found the Vernes to be charming hosts and so far enjoyed every minute of his stay. 'I had taken you for a man of science.'

'I cannot say that I was ever particularly taken with science,' Verne replied, much to Watson's astonishment. 'But I suppose I have always had a fascination for mechanics. When I was a lad I used to adore watching machines at work. My father had a country house at Chantenay, at the mouth of the Loire, and near there is the government machine factory of Indret. I never went to Chantenay without going into the factory and watching the machines at work, sometimes for hours at a time.

'This taste has remained with me all my life, and today I still have as much pleasure in watching the engine of a fine locomotive at work as I have in contemplating a picture by Raphael, say, or Correggio.'

'But do you not feel that science has added so much to our knowledge and ability?'

'It may be the answer to *some* of our problems, *Docteur*. But I am convinced that in the end it will only create new ones. In fact, my very first book was written to illustrate that very point. But my editor, who is a wise and generous man, persuaded me not to publish it, at least for the time being. And so *Paris in the Twentieth Century,* as it was called, remains locked away in his safe – for now.'

Watson blew a smoke-ring. The evening was so pleasant and peaceful that it was hard to believe he was here more as an unofficial bodyguard than a house guest. 'May I ask what you are working on at present?'

Verne organized his thoughts momentarily before saying: 'It is a story of pride, rivalry and vengeance. The central character is a mystery man called Robur, about whom little is known. However, he has invented and pilots a huge, heavier-than-air rotorcraft, which is able to fly thanks to the artful arrangement of its many propellers.

'Robur is a man of great strength and intelligence,' he continued, 'but one who is also ruled by anger and vanity. When he is rejected by his peers, he abducts a number of people and takes them aboard his craft to prove that he has indeed mastered the power of flight.'

'It sounds thrilling, sir,' said Watson, hanging on his every word. 'May I ask what it will be called?'

Verne smiled ruefully. 'There, sir, you have me. You know, I have never yet had a problem with writing, but with titles it is a different matter entirely. I agonize over them.'

'What about ... *Robur the Conqueror?*'

Verne thoughtfully considered Watson's suggestion, then nodded. 'Yes ... yes, I like it.'

'Or perhaps ... *The Clipper of the Clouds.*'

'Excellent!'

'Then you have a choice, sir. You may use one or the other.'

'Or both,' mused Verne. He winced suddenly, as his bandaged leg gave a twinge. 'You know, I am sure I must be ruining your holiday, Dr Watson.'

'Not a bit of it, sir.'

'Nevertheless, I cannot help but think that M'sieur Holmes has left you ... how would you say it? "Holding the baby"?'

Watson smiled. 'You couldn't be more wrong. Although I wish the circumstances had been different, I have truly relished this opportunity to spend time with you.'

'And it has been good for me also, to have someone like yourself to talk with,' confessed Verne. 'I make no apology for it, either. I enjoy the company of men. I always have. They make excellent travelling companions, and as you may know, I adore travel. And men of science like yourself – and a *Scotsman*, too, for I have a deep and abiding love for that country! – are the best of all.

'My wife ... she is a fine woman, but she has never read a single one of my books, and knows little of the world I inhabit ... nor indeed the loneliness I so often feel.'

'Loneliness, sir?'

'My wife was a widow when first I met her,' Verne confessed. 'She had two daughters from that earlier union and she dotes

upon them both. I, *Docteur,* have only one son, and he and I ...
I suppose you would call us *estranged.*

'He has never taken life seriously, and his cavalier attitude
has always been at odds with my own, and at times has cost
me dearly, financially as well as emotionally. Perhaps I seek
the company of men because, deep down, I really crave the
company of my son.'

Watson held his silence. There was little he could say to the
statement, and in any case sensed that the writer did not
expect a reply. He was in some way trying to unburden
himself, so Watson simply allowed him to talk uninterrupted.

'You know,' Verne continued, almost to himself, 'I am
ashamed to say that Michel's behaviour eventually forced me
to send him to the Mettray Penal Colony.'

He noticed the surprise on Watson's face and laughed
suddenly. 'No, my friend, it is not a prison as such, though the
regime is certainly hard. No – it was simply my hope that such
an ordered environment would instil self-discipline in him, but
of course it did not.

'When he was nineteen he eloped with an actress and
singer he met at our local municipal theatre. He did not do it
for love, I think. He did it expressly because I forbade the
union. But what can you do? I am close to sixty now, *Docteur.*
Next year I celebrate my thirtieth wedding anniversary, and
indeed am supposed to be celebrating the thirtieth anniversary of my first meeting with Honorine with a party at
Versailles next week.

'Sooner or later a man begins to think of his own mortality,
and realize that he must make amends while he still can. So I
swallowed my pride and gave the couple my blessing – at
which point Michel promptly abandoned his bride and took up
with another woman, this one a mere child. Sixteen, she was.
And already they have one child out of wedlock and another, I
believe, on the way.

'It seems that anything he *can* do to spite me, he *will* do. But

such is the way of things in our family.' He hesitated momentarily, then murmured: 'Insanity runs through it, you know. It
is hereditary.'

Again Watson did not reply immediately. Finally he said: 'Do
you know that for a fact, *m'sieur*?'

'Oh yes,' Verne said with sad certainty. 'I tell you all this
because I trust you, *Docteur*, and know that this conversation
will go no further. But I also tell you this for another reason. I
am afraid that if M'sieur Holmes continues to poke around in
my affairs, however laudable his motives may be, he may
somehow encourage ... speculation ... about my family that I
would prefer to avoid.'

'Holmes is the epitome of discretion, sir, I assure you.'

'Nevertheless,' Verne said, uncomfortable now, 'I would
prefer it if he were to leave this matter be. Do you think you
could persuade him to do this for me?'

'It is for you that he is investigating at all, sir.'

'And do you think he has grounds for his suspicions?'

'There you have me, M'sieur Verne. You and I may spend a
week, a month or a year looking directly at a thing and not
detect within it the things Holmes will detect in a trice. I
cannot claim to understand his convictions in this matter, but
I have no doubt that they are true.'

'Even though he has been ... unwell?'

Watson sat a little straighter. 'I am not sure what you are
implying, sir.'

'Please, *Docteur*. We are friends, and I mean no disrespect.
But facts are facts. Holmes has been ill. You yourself told us
over dinner that the purpose of this trip was to help him
convalesce. Is it not possible that he has convinced himself
that there is some dark conspiracy at work here, where in fact
there is nothing more than an unfortunate family argument
which has been blown out of all proportion?'

Watson frowned. 'It is possible, of course,' he allowed. And he
cursed himself for not having realized as much himself. But

after so many weeks spent cloistered in his room, the central player in a drug-fuelled haze, Holmes had finally come back to life. And he, Watson, had been so delighted to see it that he had not even thought to question whether or not the conspiracy to which Holmes had referred only existed within his own over-heated imagination.

'We can only await developments,' he said at last. 'But please, *m'sieur*, set your mind at rest upon one thing. Neither Holmes nor I shall do anything to besmirch your family name.'

Verne stared into the fire and muttered cryptically: 'It may already be too late for that.'

CHAPTER THIRTEEN

Jailhouse Ruck

Sergeant Bessette went off duty at four o'clock and spent the next hour or so drinking cognac at the café opposite the post and telegraph office on Rue Gambetta. It worried him that he had made such a foolish mistake that morning. He should have insisted on seeing identification before he allowed the fictitious Lucien Menard to see Gaston Verne. What worried him even more was that he knew he was in the employ of men who seldom tolerated mistakes.

At first he had feared that punishment would be swift, that the dossier they had compiled on him, listing all the bribes he had taken over the years, all the evidence he had fabricated on behalf of others to ensure that their rivals were discredited and removed from the scene, would be delivered immediately to the *Ministère de la Justice.*

He had spent the remainder of the afternoon trying to concentrate on paperwork, snapping irritable orders at the *gendarmes* around him like the condemned man he believed himself to be. But with every minute that passed, his misgivings eased. Perhaps they were going to give him another chance. If they did, he would not fail them again. He daren't.

Finally he wandered over to the post office and asked if anything had come in for Emile Devereaux, an alias his secret employers had bestowed upon him when he first went to work for them. *Non, m'sieur,* he was told. *Nothing yet.*

He went back to the café and drank more cognac. He was

drinking more and more of it lately. Around him, men and women, the girls from the school just along the road all went about their business, blissfully unaware that they had never truly been much more than puppets. Their fates, and the fate of every Frenchman, had nearly always been directed, to one degree or another, behind the scenes.

Bessette had realized this early on. And in a country where there were but two groups, the rulers and the ruled, Gabriel Bessette would side with the rulers every time.

He checked his pocket watch and sighed. He had just spent the slowest half-hour of his entire life. He got up and went back over to the post office. Was there anything for Emile Devereaux yet?

This time the clerk said yes.

He handed over the telegram and went back to work. Bessette went outside, tore open the flimsy envelope and read the artfully coded message within.

The news was both good and bad.

On the one hand, he had been given another chance to prove himself.

On the other, he had to kill a man.

He had to kill Gaston Verne.

He folded the telegram and stuffed it into his pocket. Later, at his little *appartement* in one of the city's least-underprivileged *banlieues,* he would burn it and dispose of the ashes just as he had been instructed.

Now, as he fought the urge to have one more drink and instead forced himself to walk slowly away from the café, he thought about his orders; firstly whether or not he could actually carry them out, then *when* he would carry them out, and finally ... *how* he would carry them out.

It was almost midnight when Bessette unlocked the access door set into one of the double wooden gates that led into the central police station's back yard. The city was silent, in darkness. The night was cold, and he saw his breath steaming in the faint moonlight.

He closed the door behind him and paused for a moment to listen to his surroundings. He could smell the stables, off to his left. A horse shifted, snorted and fell quiet again. To his right loomed the silhouettes of two parked wagonettes and three coaches. From where he stood, moonlight made the cobbled yard shine as if damp.

At length he moved again, this time ghosting across the yard, keeping his weight on the outer edges of his feet to minimize any sound. He reached the door in the station's rear wall and gently inserted another key from the chain attached to his belt.

With the softest of clicks, the door swung open.

He stepped into a darkened, brown-painted corridor. Around him the station was more like a mortuary. Sergeant Lepage would be manning the desk tonight. Close to retirement, he was old and fat and dozed a lot. There might be one or two *gendarmes* in the staff room, but everyone else would be out patrolling the streets.

There was a door in the facing wall. He went to it and carefully turned the dented brass-ball handle. The hinges squeaked softly and he winced, but the noise did not betray him. He peered through the crack between door and frame. A large, desk-filled room lay beyond. And yes, there was Lepage seated in a chair at the counter, his back to him, his double chin resting on his chest, his shoulders rising and falling rhythmically.

Bessette smiled grimly.

He let himself into the room, closed the door behind him and turned quickly to the right. He went through another door, descended a flight of cold stone steps and found himself in the basement cellblock. Still everything was quiet.

His heartbeat accelerating now, he hurried quietly along the corridor until he reached the cell he wanted.

This was going to rely on speed, if he was to get away with it. He could give the prisoner no chance to cry out. He had to be silenced quickly, permanently, and then Bessette had to hope he would have similar luck in leaving the station undetected.

He drew a breath. This was murder, plain and simple. But he knew also that it was kill or *be* killed. For if he failed the organization again....

He fumbled with his key ring. Suddenly his hands were trembling, his fingers stubborn and unresponsive. His breath sounded loud in his ears. His pulse raced. He'd never exactly been an angel, but neither had he ever committed murder before.

He stopped, closed his eyes, drew a deep breath. *Calm down,* he told himself. *Calm down!* After a moment, he did.

He unlocked the door, entered and closed it behind him.

The prisoner was huddled beneath his single grey blanket, snoring softly. Bessette's shadow fell across him. It took something from one pocket – something long, slim and deadly; a knife – and then drew back his arm to deliver a single killing blow.

The figure beneath the blanket seemed to explode.

The blanket flew back like a departing spirit and the man beneath it sat up fast. Bessette caught a bewildering flicker of movement, and then something cold poked him hard in the sternum, keeping him at bay.

It was the brass ferrule of a cane.

'Give it up, *m'sieur!*' snapped a voice that did not belong to Gaston Verne.

Bessette cursed himself for being a fool. No wonder it had been so easy to get in; the whole thing was a trap – and he had walked right into it!

Desperation boiled up in him and he lashed out, knocking the cane aside. At the same time he whirled around and lunged for the door. His intended target, the man he had believed to be Gaston Verne, sprang up from the cot and brought the cane down on his forearm as he reached for the door. Pain sawed through him. He yelped, turned and threw himself at his opponent.

For an indeterminate time they grappled, each struggling to get the upper hand. Bessette's knife was knocked from his fingers and fell clattering on the stone floor. Cursing, he punched wildly at his opponent's head and missed. His opponent pushed him away. Bessette slammed against the opposite wall. Breath knocked out of him, he lunged forward again in a desperate charge.

The other man came to meet him. Just before they collided, he half-turned so that he led with his shoulder. Then, crouching slightly, he deftly thrust his shoulder into Bessette's armpit and twisted quickly at the waist.

Bessette went over the other man's shoulder and crashed heavily to the floor. All the air was knocked out of him and stars popped in the darkness before his eyes.

Gasping, he rolled over onto his hands and knees. The other man crouched over him. Regaining his wind, Bessette was about to launch himself back into the fray when the cell door flew open. He froze, suddenly illuminated by the gaslight that brightened the corridor outside.

Inspector Mathes barked: 'Bessette! Don't move, man, or I'll shoot!'

Bessette, seeing the 12mm single-action Galand revolver in Mathes's hand, grudgingly obeyed.

The inspector glanced across at Bessette's opponent, the man who had posed as Gaston Verne, and said: 'Good work, M'sieur Holmes. It seems I was right to trust your judgement in this matter, after all.'

CHAPTER FOURTEEN

Orange Blossom, Lavender and Honeysuckle

The darkly handsome police inspector flopped into the chair behind his messy desk and heaved a heartfelt sigh. It had been a long night, but not necessarily a profitable one. He looked at Holmes, who was seated in the visitor's chair across from him, and said: 'There can be no doubt about it; there is indeed more to this affair than seemed obvious at the outset. But Bessette – *Bessette,* of all people, the very last man I would have expected to double as an assassin! – isn't going to talk any time soon. He has made that all too clear.'

Mathes had been understandably sceptical when Holmes had first intercepted him as he left the police station at dusk. Anxious to keep their meeting secret, Holmes had asked if they might speak in private. When the puzzled policeman agreed, he had taken him to Amiens Cathedral, the most public and yet at the same time private place he could think of.

The cathedral was one of the city's most imposing sights, and certainly the tallest in all of France. Construction had started in 1220, following a fire that destroyed its predecessor at the same location, and now, in addition to being a place of worship, it also contained works of art and decoration that had been accumulated over the seventy years it had taken to build.

At that time of the early evening, the church was largely deserted. Holmes looked around to make sure no one was watching them, then led Mathes into the Chapel of St Thomas of Canterbury. They sat beside each other on a pew facing the impressive altar, and it was here that Holmes confided his suspicions.

'I have great respect for you and your methods, *m'sieur*,' Mathes replied softly once Holmes had finished, 'but this time I think you may be mistaken, for the very simple reason that Gaston Verne himself has at last confessed his motive … well, after a fashion, at least.'

Holmes was immediately attentive. 'What did he say?'

Mathes hesitated. 'I can rely upon your discretion?'

'Of course.'

'He blamed "family affairs of such sensitivity that I am unable to divulge them". His exact words.'

'And that was *all* he said?'

'He would be drawn no further, *m'sieur*.'

'Nevertheless, I must ask you to indulge me, Inspector. It is my conviction that Gaston Verne was somehow "primed" by person or persons unknown to make the attempt upon his uncle's life. Those same perpetrators might make another attempt, not only upon Jules Verne but also his nephew.'

'Why the nephew?'

'Because Gaston is a link to them, and may even be privy to their true motive. He has already given me what may or may not be a vital clue, and since he is mentally unstable, they cannot guarantee that he will not, sooner or later, tell all.'

Mathes frowned for a moment, his mind racing. Then he said: 'I should find it most embarrassing to be made a fool of, *m'sieur*. But equally, I should find it most embarrassing to lose a prisoner in my care.'

'Then you'll give me the benefit of the doubt?'

Mathes nodded grimly. 'Where do you suggest we begin?'

'Firstly, we must exercise extreme discretion. We do not know yet who else is involved, or where they are, or what they will do next. May I rely upon *your* discretion?'

'Of course.'

'I thought as much. Inspector, this is what I have in mind.'

So it was that Mathes, acting entirely alone and without official sanction, had removed Gaston Verne from one cell and placed him in the one next door. And so it was that he smuggled Holmes into the building shortly thereafter and allowed him to take Gaston's place. After that there was nothing to do but watch and wait.

'But Bessette, of all people,' Mathes said, taking a cigarette from a packet on his cluttered desk. 'I never much cared for the man, but I never thought him capable of murder.'

'That, I fear, is one of the problems,' Holmes said. 'There is no way to tell just whom we may trust. If the people behind the attempt on Verne's life are as powerful as I suspect, they probably have agents everywhere.'

'At least now we have two leads to them – Gaston and Bessette.'

'Yes. But as you rightly said just now, Bessette is not about to betray them.'

At first, as they handcuffed him, the brawny sergeant had tried to protest his innocence. He claimed to have returned to the station simply to check on the prisoner. But the dropped knife, together with Holmes's testimony to the contrary, was damning; and when Bessette realized it, he refused to make any further comment, other than to demand a lawyer.

'I'm not getting anyone out of bed at this time of night for your benefit,' Mathes replied harshly. He gestured for the two *gendarmes* who had witnessed the interrogation to take their sergeant away. 'You can see your lawyer in the morning.'

'There is just one other thing,' Holmes had added.

Bessette gave him a surly glare.

'What do the letters *VDC* stand for?'

Bessette's bloodshot eyes betrayed his surprise, but only for an instant. Then he replied in a low growl: 'I have no idea.'

*

'Nevertheless,' Holmes now continued to Mathes, 'he will talk sooner or later. The prospect of a meeting with *Madame la Guillotine* can be a powerful persuader.'

Mathes blew smoke towards the ceiling. 'And if nothing else, at least we have confirmed your suspicion that there is more to this business than first appeared.'

Holmes stood and gathered his hat and cane. 'Well, I fear we will accomplish little more tonight, Inspector.'

'*Non.* But I will have another crack at Bessette in the morning, and let you know the minute I learn anything.'

'Thank you.' They shook hands. 'Good night.'

Holmes left the building the same way Bessette had entered it; by way of the back yard. The night was still quiet but for the distant yapping of a prowling dog. Holmes knew he'd be lucky to find a cab at this late hour, and resigned himself to the long walk back to the Hotel Couronne. As soon as he stepped out onto Rue de la Republique, however, he thought he glimpsed a movement in the mouth of an alleyway across the road – a figure, startled by his sudden appearance, hurriedly backing into the shadows there.

Holmes stopped and peered closer, but saw nothing and decided he had been mistaken.

And yet....

And yet his instincts told him beyond all doubt that he was being watched.

On impulse he crossed the road and headed directly towards the alleyway, the tip of his cane tapping briskly against the cobbles.

He was halfway there when whoever was lurking in the shadows made a run for it. Holmes recognized the unmistakable sound of high heels and realized for the first time that his watcher was a woman.

He broke into a run, knowing that she might well be nothing more than a lady of the night, afraid of arrest, but knowing also that he could not take the chance in case she was actually something much more.

He entered the alleyway just as she reached its farthest end and vanished around the corner. In that instant he saw a woman in – it was difficult to be sure in the uncertain yellow glow of the streetlamps, but he thought it was a purple outfit. He went after her. But he had only taken a few steps when suddenly the whole world began to undulate and melt around him.

The part of his mind that still worked told him that the effects of opiate withdrawal were once again coursing through him. He cursed his luck even as he broke stride and slumped hard against a cold stone wall. He closed his eyes, hugged himself, set his teeth. He was wracked by shivers even though he burned inside. After a few more seconds the sensation reached such a pitch that he almost forgot who and where he was –

And then, mercifully, the rushing in his ears began to recede, he felt the attack passing, passing ... and shivered.

Gradually he returned to his senses and forced himself to walk unsteadily to the far end of the alley. He knew the woman would be long gone by now, but hoped she had left something identifiable behind.

The cold night air was permeated with her scent: orange blossom, lavender and honeysuckle.

He had smelled those same fragrances before somewhere, and recently. But where?

Who was she? he wondered. What had she been doing there in a darkened alleyway in the small hours of a chilly March morning? Was she another part of the puzzle he was attempting to solve?

He had the strongest possible conviction that she was.

CHAPTER FIFTEEN

———— ❧ ————

The Suicide Tree

A little before ten o'clock the following morning Holmes, who habitually slept late, was woken rudely by an urgent tapping at his hotel room door. At once he threw on his red dressing gown and answered it.

Facing him was an apologetic desk clerk holding out an envelope upon which was written his name. 'I am sorry to disturb you, *m'sieur,* but this just came for you. The boy said it was urgent.'

Holmes took the envelope with a perfunctory nod of thanks and closed the door. He opened the envelope and quickly scanned its contents. The note read simply:

Monsieur Holmes,
Please come at once. Bessette found dead in cell this
morning.
Mathes

The tightening of his thin lips was his only reaction to the news.

Stuffing the note into his pocket, he quickly saw to his ablutions, then scribbled a message for Watson and made arrangements at the desk for a boy to deliver it to Rue de Charles Dubois. He then left the hotel, hailed a cab and went directly to the police station.

Mathes was waiting for him at the front desk when he

arrived. The inspector's tone was as grim as his manner. 'Come this way, *m'sieur.*' He quickly led Holmes to the cells below ground. 'I have left everything just as we found it. Nothing has been touched or disturbed.'

'Good man.'

Mathes unlocked the cell and they went inside. The small room – an almost exact replica of the one in which Holmes had first interviewed Gaston – was airless and smelled sourly of vomit. Bessette lay crookedly across the cot, his eyes half-closed and very slightly crossed. His fists were clenched.

'What happened?' asked Holmes, bending to examine the dead man.

'As you know, he wanted to see a lawyer, a man he named as Prideaux. The man was sent for. He arrived. They conversed briefly in this very cell. The guard who let Prideaux out at the end of the interview reports that Bessette was in good spirits. Then, about an hour later he started hammering on the cell door, saying he had stomach pains. The guard ignored him at first, thinking that Bessette was trying to fool him into unlocking the cell and letting him out. When the hammering abruptly stopped a few minutes later, he looked in through the eye-hole you see in the door here. Bessette had vomited, collapsed upon the cot and fallen into some kind of coma. Medical aid was summoned immediately, but by the time the doctor arrived Bessette was dead.'

'He has been examined by your judicial surgeon?'

'*Oui.* Cause of death appears to be a thrombosis.'

'Did he have any history of heart disease?'

'Not to my knowledge, no. We can check with the man's own physician.'

'Do so,' Holmes replied vaguely, glancing around the room. 'Have you ever heard of this man Prideaux?'

'No. But I sent a man to fetch him from the address Bessette gave us—'

'—and when he got there, the bird had flown,' guessed Holmes.

'Exactly.'

'Then it seems we have a simple case of murder on our hands,' said Holmes. 'We may assume with some confidence that Prideaux was one of Bessette's confederates in this enterprise. When he was caught trying to murder Gaston Verne, Bessette demanded to see his "lawyer". In reality I suspect that Prideaux was also in the employ of Bessette's masters. He called upon this man for help, most probably to orchestrate a means by which he could make good his escape.'

'But instead this man killed him in cold blood?' Mathes asked sceptically.

'Certainly. As we already know, Inspector, these people do not draw the line at murder. Besides, this man Bessette had become another liability. He had to be removed before he could be tempted to turn state's evidence.'

'But ... how did it happen? The surgeon says his heart gave out.'

'Clearly he was poisoned. Prideaux offered him a flask of brandy, perhaps to celebrate his own empty promise of arranging Bessette's escape. You can smell the spirit upon the dead man's lips. Bessette was only too happy to accept. The man was a drinker, as you know.'

'I'm sorry, *m'sieur,* but I knew no such thing.'

'Then I suggest you examine the man more closely. The diagnosis of medical conditions is more the speciality of my colleague, Dr Watson, but I know a drinker when I see one. The man's yellowish pallor, the spider-like veins on his nose and cheeks, the redness of his palms, the premature loss of hair colour, which is suggestive of an imbalance of copper and zinc.'

'Very well. I accept that he might have been a drinker. But what about Prideaux's use of a hip flask?'

'They sat at this table when they spoke,' said Holmes with a gesture. 'See here in the fine film of dust, there is the faintest outline of a gently curved shape approximately five inches long and perhaps three-quarters of an inch wide. This is where Prideaux set the hip-flask down.'

'Then we truly are dealing with ruthless men.'

'And clever ones,' Holmes said admiringly. 'My feeling is that a further examination of the body in order to identify the poison used will be of no use. Not for these people the common-place arsenic or potassium chloride.'

'Why not?'

'Because Prideaux did not want his man to become ill or die until he was well on his way out of Amiens. As you have already noted, Bessette did not become ill until an hour after Prideaux had left. Now, arsenic can be used to kill slowly, but only in small doses administered over a long period of time. As for potassium chloride, I believe an impractical amount, perhaps eight or ten ounces – forgive me, Inspector; let us say a little over two hundred grams – would be required to kill a man of Bessette's size.

'Based upon the facts as you have recounted them, however, I lean toward an altogether more ingenious method, namely the fruit of *Cerbera odollam* – the so-called suicide tree.'

Mathes's frown deepened. 'I am sorry, *m'sieur*, but again you have lost me.'

'*Cerbera odollam*, also known as the Pong-pong or Othalanga, is a tree that flourishes throughout south-east Asia and India. Its fruit yields a potent poison that disrupts the heartbeat and mimics the symptoms of a thrombosis. It is not especially difficult to extract; the fruit is simply chopped into small pieces and its poison extracted in a solution of methanol by a method known as cold soaking. Bessette presented all the symptoms of this particular poison. It took about an hour to work on him. He suffered abdominal pain, he vomited, his heartbeat slowed and finally he lapsed into a coma.'

'And he never suspected a thing?'

'Obviously not. It is true that the poison has a somewhat bitter taste, but the strong brandy would have disguised that.

Bessette was finished the minute he took that celebratory drink.'

Mathes ran his fingers through his curly black hair. 'These people must be stopped at all costs.'

'Of course. But until we know their true motive, where do we begin?'

'Prideaux is the obvious answer.'

'Prideaux will be long gone by now, Inspector. And my feeling is that wherever he goes, he will lie low until this entire business dies down. However, it can do no harm to circulate the man's description to the surrounding *départements*.'

'And in the meantime?'

'In the meantime, Inspector,' Holmes said forcefully, 'I should be most grateful if you would guard Gaston Verne with your very life.'

CHAPTER SIXTEEN

Something to Hide

Holmes left the police station and took a cab directly to Verne's house. Watson answered the bell with the spaniel, Follet, growling warily by his side. Relaxing visibly when he saw Holmes through one of the conservatory hall windows, Watson dropped his old service revolver back into his jacket pocket and quickly opened the door.

'What has happened, Holmes? Your note told me to be on my guard.'

'In a moment, Watson. All is well here, I trust?'

'As quiet as a—'

'—graveyard?' finished Holmes. 'Where is Verne?'

'Upstairs, writing.'

'I must see him at once.'

Honorine was waiting in the hallway, an anxious look on her face. 'Has something happened, *m'sieur*?' she asked as Holmes approached. 'When the boy came with your note—'

'There has been a development,' he said.

'Something to do with Gaston?' she asked, almost fearfully.

'Indirectly, *madame*. Now, if you will be so kind as to join your husband, I need only explain everything the once.'

She nodded and turned to a door on her left. Watson hurried to open it for them, and revealed a circular staircase beyond. He and Holmes followed Honorine up to a small but well-appointed set of rooms, outside the smallest of which Verne stood leaning on his crutches.

'M'sieur Holmes,' he cried. 'What news is there? Is Gaston—?'

'He is safe and well,' Holmes assured him.

'Thank God!' breathed Verne.

He ushered them all into the small room behind him, which was clearly his workroom. Two cluttered wooden desks sat beneath a window that offered a spectacular view of the slender spire of Amiens Cathedral. Behind it Holmes noticed a small camp-bed and frowned. Catching his expression, Verne explained self-consciously: 'I begin work every morning at five. By eleven I have to rest.'

The room was bare of all ornamentation save for two busts, one of Molière, the other of Shakespeare, and a watercolour of a yacht known as the *St Michel III*.

Verne gestured to another door. 'Please, come through to the library.'

The library was a much bigger room, in the centre of which sat a large table stacked high with newspapers and periodicals. Nearby, a set of little cardboard pigeonholes was jammed tight with the notes Verne habitually kept on almost every subject.

'Now, sir,' Verne said grimly as Honorine slipped her arm fondly under his. 'What has happened?'

'I believe there can no longer be any doubt that your life is at risk,' Holmes said gravely. 'Someone, somewhere means you harm, M'sieur Verne. They broke your nephew out of the sanatorium where he had been placed and by the most sadistic of means convinced him to kill you upon their behalf. When that failed, an attempt was made to eliminate Gaston – an attempt Inspector Mathes and I were able to foil last night. But the man who tried to kill Gaston was himself murdered this very morning.'

Honorine paled at the revelation. Verne and Watson exchanged a glance. Clearly this affair could no longer be dismissed as a product of Holmes's imagination.

'Someone wants you dead, M'sieur Verne,' Holmes

continued, 'and they are determined and ruthless enough to cover their tracks by any means possible. Are you sure you cannot think of anyone who might want to hurt you?'

'No.'

'No one with the initials "V.D.C,"?'

'No, *m'sieur*.'

'Need I assure you that anything you choose to tell us will be held in the strictest confidence?'

'I appreciate that, but … I cannot think of any reason why anyone should want to kill me.'

'However … *sensitive* … that reason might be?'

A nerve in Verne's face twitched at Holmes's use of the word. 'I am not sure what you are implying, *m'sieur*,' he said stiffly.

'I believe you are, sir. I believe you know *exactly* what I am implying. What's more, it will make this investigation go easier if you confide in us.'

Verne reddened. Then, pulling away from his wife, he leaned on his crutches and crossed the room to a window. 'There are some things a man must keep to himself, M'sieur Holmes.'

'Even if by doing so he condemns himself to death? Condemns his *nephew* to death? Allows the perpetrators of the crime to go unpunished?'

'*Oui*. Even then,' Verne said stubbornly.

Holmes squared his shoulders. 'Nevertheless, sir, we must take every step to guard you until the enemy is brought to book – at which time whatever you choose to withhold from us now may well become public knowledge whether you wish it or not.'

'What do you suggest?' asked Honorine. 'We will cooperate as much as we can. All I ask – all *we* ask – is that you do everything in your power to protect Jules's good name.'

'Then I strongly advise that we begin by moving Gaston to a nursing home, the location of which will be known only to us and your most trusted friends,' said Holmes. 'Until this is over, he is a target, too, and we must afford him every protection.'

'Of course,' Verne agreed. 'But that is a decision only his father, my brother Paul, can make.'

'Where does he live, M'sieur Verne?'

'Nantes. I will send a telegram at once—'

'We dare not risk that, I am afraid. A telegram could easily be intercepted.'

Verne's eyes widened. 'Do you really believe that these people, whoever they are, would attempt such a thing?'

'They are powerful, and they are everywhere,' Holmes replied simply, 'and because of that we cannot take the risk that they will *not* intercept it. No – it will be better if I visit your brother in person, and explain everything to him face to face.'

'You will not possibly be able to make the return trip in one day,' said Honorine.

'I will stay over and return either tomorrow or the day after, depending upon where my subsequent inquiries take me. Now, if you will excuse me, I will return to my hotel, collect some things and then make my way to Nantes. If you will supply me with a letter of introduction, *m'sieur…?*'

'At once.'

'*Merçi.* As soon as I have an answer from your brother, I will wire you with a simple yes or no.'

Watson said: 'Come, Holmes. I'll walk you downstairs while M'sieur Verne prepares his letter.'

When they were back in the conservatory hall he added quietly: 'Have a care, old chap. You are here to convalesce, remember.'

'I am fine, Watson. Never better.'

'Still … how have you been, in yourself? You look somewhat pale.'

'It is nothing. I feel *energized,* old friend. Truly, I could ask for nothing more.'

'Well, as I say, have a care, Holmes. You have been quite desperately ill, whether you choose to believe it or not. Don't try to run before you can walk.'

Shortly, Honorine came downstairs and handed Holmes an envelope, upon which Verne himself had scribbled his brother's name and address. 'God speed, M'sieur Holmes,' she said.

Watson extended his hand. 'And remember what I said, Holmes.'

'I will, old friend.' They shook hands. 'But have a care for *yourself,* too, Watson. I still believe you will find more danger here than I will in Nantes.'

CHAPTER SEVENTEEN

Paul Verne

A five-hour train journey brought Holmes south and west to Nantes just before dusk. He stood on the platform for a moment, checking the faces of the debarking passengers. He recognized no one. Satisfied that he hadn't been followed, he headed for the exit.

As he stepped out of the Grand Gare, the setting sun threw a garland of orange and gold, pale pink and powder blue across the darkening sky. He hailed a cab and asked to be taken to the address Jules Verne had supplied.

The journey proved to be illuminating. Nantes was a vibrant, progressive city settled on the banks of the River Loire, where the Rivers Sèvre Nantaise and Erdre met to form the Loire's left and right tributaries. Though it was no longer the major commercial port it had once been, ocean-going ships could still be seen navigating their way inland from the Atlantic, which lay no more than fifty kilometres south.

At length Holmes reached his destination: a double row of connected, three-storey, grey-stone houses with wrought-iron balconies on a narrow, cobbled street that wound its way up a gentle incline. Holmes double-checked the address Honorine had given him, paused before a tall red-painted front door and knocked.

Paul Verne answered after a brief wait. Holmes introduced himself and explained briefly why he was there. Though surprised to find himself talking to a detective of Holmes's repute, Paul invited him in and led him into a dimly lit, modestly furnished sitting room. There, he offered Holmes a glass of port, which Holmes graciously refused, and then excused himself to notify his wife that they had a guest.

He returned shortly, sat on a sofa facing Holmes and the two men began to talk. Studying him, Holmes estimated that Paul was a year or so younger than his brother and only vaguely resembled Jules. His hair was thick and dark, worn with a left-side part. He had direct eyes, a slightly hooked nose, full sideburns, a thick moustache and a chin-beard.

Though he was a stockbroker by trade, Holmes knew that he shared something of his brother's creative streak. He dabbled in writing and composing, but his real love had always been the sea. Unfortunately, fragile health had denied him the mariner's life he had so desired.

Not that he showed any bitterness about it. In temperament he was far more cheerful than his somewhat dour, pessimistic brother, and though he and his wife, Berthe – a rather cheerless younger woman who now entered – treated Holmes warily at first, Paul's attitude thawed rapidly once he read Jules's letter of introduction.

'Jules speaks highly of you, M'sieur Holmes, and with no small justification. How is he? *Really,* I mean. Was he *badly* wounded?'

'He will limp for the rest of his days,' Holmes replied. 'But the matter could have been worse.'

Paul nodded. 'I am, of course, familiar with your reputation, and can only thank you for the service you have already performed for my family. Saving Gaston's life … well, that is not something I am likely to forget. I am in your debt, sir, so please – ask of me what you will.'

'The matter is a simple one, *m'sieur.* For reasons I do not yet fully understand, I believe your son has become an unwitting participant in a plot to kill your brother. Fortunately, the murder attempt failed. But then Gaston himself became a

target, and it is my conviction that whoever is behind the plot
will make another attempt to silence him. Therefore, I am here
to ask your permission to take him from his prison cell in
Amiens and hide him away until the matter is resolved.'

Though shocked by the news, Paul said without hesitation:
'Of course.' But before he could say more he stopped, choked by
emotion, and quickly turned his face away. Holmes waited
patiently, half-expecting Berthe to make some attempt to
comfort her husband. She did not.

After a few moments Paul cleared his throat and turned
back to him. His dark eyes still swam with tears. 'Forgive me,
m'sieur, but I am just relieved to know that Gaston did not
take it upon himself to attempt murder – that he was forced
into it.'

'How is he?' asked Berthe.

'He has withdrawn into himself, I'm afraid.'

'Who made him do this dreadful thing?' asked Paul.

'That is what I am still trying to find out,' said Holmes, adding:
'I believe Gaston has a history of … emotional problems?'

'Yes. But that was not always the case. He is the eldest of
our four children, and a brilliant scholar, but sometimes brilliance can be as much a curse as a blessing.'

Holmes offered no comment, but knew only too well how
true the statement was. 'Your brother also speaks highly of
him,' he said.

'That is no surprise, *m'sieur.* Jules spent much time with the
boy, more even than I. And Gaston was never happier than
when he was in Jules's company. In my brother he found an
intellectual match, someone with whom he felt … comfortable.
Jules took him around the world, even arranged a very good
job for him in Paris. Unfortunately, somewhere along the way
…' His voice faltered. '*M'sieur,* are you *sure* I can rely upon
your confidence?'

'I give you my word.'

'Then please judge neither Gaston, nor Jules, nor indeed me, too harshly. But it seemed to me that Gaston became ... possessive of Jules – even jealous when not in his company.'

'Did you ever mention this to your son?'

'Once.'

'How did he react?'

'He became quite angry with me. He said I was imagining things.' Paul sighed, troubled. 'To be honest with you, M'sieur Holmes, I found his actions distressing since I felt that the emotion was wholly ... unnatural.'

Betraying nothing, Holmes said: 'Did Jules do anything to encourage this behaviour?'

'I do not like to think so. In any case, I felt uncomfortable with the relationship and requested that Jules distance himself from Gaston. This he did, though I know it pained him greatly to end their friendship.

'As for Gaston, he was distraught. It was this, I believe, that finally unhinged him. He grew belligerent, complained that he was constantly being followed by the police and began to talk of going to live in England. Eventually he had a nervous breakdown and we had no choice but to admit him to a sanatorium in Blois.'

'And it was from this sanatorium that he escaped?'

'Yes.'

After a pause Holmes said quietly: 'Do the initials "V.D.C." mean anything to you, *m'sieur?*'

Paul thought for a moment. 'I am sorry. They mean nothing.'

'Do you keep any pistols, sir?'

'I have a shotgun which I use occasionally for pheasant, partridge and dove, but no. No pistols.'

'Has Gaston ever shown any interest in guns?'

'No. He was always an aesthete, M'sieur Holmes, in the very truest sense of the word. From an early age he cultivated an unusually high sensitivity to all that was beautiful in art and nature. He found violence abhorrent. He was truly the "Dreamy Mouse" Jules always called him.'

'And yet you said just now that he grew belligerent.'

'He did, and it was wholly out of character. When the mood was upon him, however, he would challenge anyone and everyone to a duel. But his weapon of choice was always the sword.'

Holmes pondered for a moment. 'If it is possible,' he said then, 'I would like to examine Gaston's room at the sanatorium, and see for myself how he escaped. Would you write me a letter of introduction, giving me the authority to do that?'

Paul shrugged. 'If it will help.'

'It may.' Holmes abruptly got to his feet. 'Well, thank you, M'sieur Verne, you and your wife have been most helpful. Before I go, however, I have one final question.'

'Ask it.'

'Does your brother have any enemies that you know of?'

'None,' Paul replied. But then his face clouded and he said, almost to himself: 'But then, I do not know everything about him.'

Holmes left Paul Verne's residence and got directions for the telegraph office on Quai Brancas. Here he sent a terse message for the attention of Dr John H. Watson, in care of Number 2 Rue Charles Dubois, Amiens:

ANSWER IS YES STOP PLEASE ARRANGE WITH ALL DISPATCH STOP

———e·ɔ———

A Busy Day

The following morning Watson took the telegram directly to Jules Verne, who was at his desk overlooking the cathedral, trying vainly to concentrate on his writing. 'I'm sorry to disturb you, sir,' he said, 'but I thought you would like to know that your brother has agreed to let us hide Gaston away until this matter is resolved.'

Verne read the telegram and nodded. 'You are not disturbing me, *Docteur*. I have read this same page at least three times without taking in a single word.'

'Have heart, sir. Everything will soon get back to normal.'

'I suppose so,' sighed Verne. 'But to more important matters; how do you propose to spirit Gaston out of Amiens? And if these "enemies" of mine are as powerful as M'sieur Holmes suggests, how can we guarantee that they will not follow you?'

'My place is by your side. Holmes has, after all, entrusted me with your safety.'

'Then we must wait for Holmes to return.'

'I do not think we dare wait. Holmes said we should act with all dispatch.' Watson thought for a moment. 'I wonder if we dare entrust Inspector Mathes with the task? We know we can trust him.'

'True. But he has a job to do here in Amiens. He cannot just drop everything to undertake a favour for the likes of us – and certainly not without arousing suspicion.'

'Is there anyone you feel you could trust?'

'Normally I would have said my publisher, Pierre-Jules Hetzel. He is a man I would trust with my life. But unfortunately he is gravely ill. In fact, his doctors do not expect him to last out the week.'

'There must be *someone*.'

Verne considered briefly, then managed to smile. 'I believe I have the very man, *Docteur*. His name is Gaspard-Felix Tourachon, though he is better known under the alias "Felix Nadar".'

Watson frowned. 'Should I have heard of him, *m'sieur*?'

'It is quite likely,' Verne said. 'Did you by any chance see the deathbed photograph of Victor Hugo that appeared in the papers last year?'

'Yes, I did.'

'Felix was the photographer. He is something of a polymath, *Docteur*. Not just a gifted photographer but also a journalist, a cartoonist and many other things besides. I have known him for more than twenty years. The man is absolutely fearless, and utterly trustworthy.'

'Where do we find him?'

'In Marseilles.'

Surprised, Watson said: 'Marseilles! That's on the other side of the country, isn't it? It overlooks the Mediterranean! It must be at least eight hundred kilometres away.'

'Closer to a thousand, I fancy.'

'With respect, sir, we need someone rather closer than that, I fear.'

'Nevertheless,' Verne said determinedly, 'he is our man. Come, *Docteur*, there is much to do if we are to make this thing work. First we must enlist Nadar's assistance. Then I think I should see my own doctor, ostensibly about this troublesome leg wound of mine, but in reality to find a safe place where Gaston can be held and treated.'

He struggled to his feet and reached for his crutches.

Watching him with concern, Watson said: 'Are you sure you want to take so much upon yourself, M'sieur Verne?'

'Anything is better than sitting here and brooding,' the author replied with feeling. 'Besides, I owe it to Gaston. He is of my blood, *Docteur,* and someone has taken him and corrupted him and attempted to use him against me. I do not take kindly to that. Nor will I stand for it. Now, if you would be so kind, my friend, please ask Honorine if she will have my carriage made ready. Then we will set to work.'

Verne was as good as his word. The coach took them to the post and telegraph office on Rue Gambetta. Here Verne sent a telegram to Felix Nadar, saying only that he needed Nadar's assistance in an urgent personal matter. He also added the phrase *'Six-Quatre'* to the message.

Watson frowned. 'What does that mean, *m'sieur?*'

Verne smiled. 'Felix will know.'

Their next stop was the surgery of Verne's doctor, where the author made a great show of hobbling painfully through the crowded waiting room. Behind closed doors, however, he dropped the pretence and came directly to the point.

'I need your help, Simonet, and I rely upon your oath to keep what we discuss here between us.'

The doctor frowned and looked from Verne to Watson and back again. *'Naturellement.* What is the problem, Jules?'

Verne told him as much as he felt the doctor needed to know. When he was finished the doctor said: 'There is a small, exclusive sanatorium just outside Le Combeau that I believe would suit your needs. It is fairly isolated and they have an excellent reputation. But I warn you, it is expensive.'

'No matter,' said Verne. 'Can I rely upon you to arrange for my nephew to be admitted?'

'Of course.'

'Then please, I beg you, offer up an alias so that we may keep this thing as quiet as we can.'

'I will see to it, and have all the details delivered to you by this afternoon.'

'I cannot explain why,' Verne said, 'but I would prefer you to handle this matter yourself. It may sound melodramatic, but you must entrust this matter to no one else, Simonet.'

They returned to the telegram office on Rue Gambetta and Verne collected a reply from Felix Nadar. It said simply:

JUST TELL ME WHEN AND WHERE STOP

Their next stop was the central police station on Rue de la Republique, where they were immediately shown into Inspector Mathes's office.

'In light of the attempt made upon my nephew's life two nights ago,' said Verne, 'Sherlock Holmes feels that we should remove Gaston to a safer location known only to a few of us, and I can only agree. But we cannot do this without your help, Inspector.'

Mathes said immediately: 'You have it, M'sieur Verne. I have only been holding him pending instructions from his family. When do you propose to take him?'

'Tonight, at midnight. Can you arrange it?'

'I will hand him over to you myself,' the inspector said. 'I have the greatest admiration for you, M'sieur Verne. To decide against pressing charges against the man who shot you and then to help him as you are doing now ... well, you are a humanitarian, sir, and I salute that. Would you care to see Gaston while you are here?'

Verne shook his head, and looked down at the tips of his shoes. 'I think not. He was – is – a dear boy. It is too painful now for me to see what his tormentors have made of him.'

There was a brief, awkward silence. Then Watson took Verne by the arm and, thanking the inspector, they left the station.

For the third time that day they stopped at the post office and Verne asked the clerk if he might consult an atlas. After a few moments of hurried calculation, he finally scribbled a new message and had it sent to Felix Nadar. It read simply:

00:00 STOP 49° 53'39.45" N STOP 2° 14'19.81" E STOP

Looking over Verne's shoulder, Watson said: 'Forgive me, but am I to understand that you expect M'sieur Nadar to be here by midnight? From Marseilles?'

'Oh, yes,' Verne replied confidently. 'He will be here.'

Watson had trouble believing him but decided not to press the issue. 'And now, sir?' he asked.

'Now, *Docteur,* let us go and get something to eat. There is a café just across the street, and their pastries are excellent. But don't take my word for it. Let us go there now.'

CHAPTER NINETEEN

Lydie

Jules Verne was right – the pastries were indeed excellent. But as it turned out, the company proved to be even better.

'I am very much a product of my times,' Verne admitted, watching as the people of Amiens walked past. 'I was born and raised in Nantes, an exciting city even then, and watching the ships on the Loire, wondering where they had come from and where they were going, inspired my love of travel and adventure.

'I was also lucky to have Brutus de Villeroi as one of my teachers at college. He went on to create the American navy's first submarine, you know – the USS *Alligator*. And of course, this too had a profound effect upon me.

'I sometimes think I was born with the urge to write, to perform in some way, to entertain. When I went to Paris to study law, I spent more time writing operettas than anything else. My father, himself a lawyer, was furious when he found out, and without his financial support I had no choice but to abandon my writings and find work. I became a stockbroker, and a moderately successful one, but my heart was always in writing, just as I suppose my head has always been in the clouds.'

He smiled wistfully and muttered: 'How sad it is when a father finds only disappointment in his son.'

Just then a shadow fell across the table and when Watson looked up, the breath caught in his throat. Standing before them was the woman who had complimented him upon his French just a few days before. Today she was wearing a three-quarter-length jacket over a snow-white blouse, and a full, ankle-length skirt in dark burgundy, her ensemble complemented by an ornate straw boater.

At once he sprang to his feet and inclined his head courteously. *'Bonjour, mademoiselle.* It is a great pleasure to see you again.'

'I am so sorry to bother you, gentlemen,' she said somewhat self-consciously. 'But I have been awaiting the chance to speak with you, M'sieur Verne, and seeing you here at this moment, quite by chance ... well, it was too good an opportunity to resist.'

Verne clearly did not wish to be interrupted, but he was nothing if not a gentleman. 'You will forgive me, *mademoiselle,* but the last few days have been something of a trial for me—'

'I know,' she replied. 'I arrived in Amiens the very day you were shot. Indeed, I was just approaching your house when it happened. I ... It was terrible. Thank goodness you were on hand, *m'sieur,'* she said to Watson, who shrugged modestly. 'I did not realize at the time that you were a doctor, but it is fortunate for M'sieur Verne here that you were.' She hesitated briefly before adding: 'You *are* John Watson, are you not? The man who records the exploits of M'sieur Sherlock Holmes?'

'I have that privilege,' said Watson.

'Then I am doubly fortunate. But please, forgive me. I can only blame my lack of manners upon my excitement at meeting not one but two great literary figures. My name is Lydie Denier. I am a journalist. Well, that is to say, I am *trying* to become a journalist. But it is not so easy for a woman. At present I write for *L'Amoureaux des Livres,* a small-circulation literary magazine in Paris. In order to prove my worth, my editor has challenged me to produce an interview with a major literary figure. I had settled upon you, M'sieur Verne, and was on my way to request it when the, ah, unfortunate situation happened. Now I see an opportunity to return to Paris with not one but two interviews!'

'I am sorry, Mademoiselle Denier, but this is not the best time,' said Verne.

'Such a shame,' she said, disappointed. 'But of course, I understand.'

Verne and Watson exchanged a look. She had seemed so enthusiastic, and of course she was so pretty....

Verne relented. 'Let us see what the morrow brings,' he suggested. 'You obviously know where I live. Come at, say, two o'clock, and we will try to oblige you with some useful quotes.'

Her face lit up. 'Oh, thank you, *messieurs*! You have no idea what this means to me!'

'*De rien,*' Watson said gallantly.

He took her hand, kissed it and looked into her eyes. He was pleased to see that she did not blush or look away. Instead she smiled fetchingly.

Delighted, he remained standing as she walked away. A lingering breeze flooded his senses with her perfume. She smelled of orange blossom, lavender and honeysuckle, and he found the combination as intoxicating as the woman herself.

CHAPTER TWENTY

Intruder

By the time they got back to Rue Charles Dubois it was late afternoon and Verne was beginning to tire. It had been a busy day and he looked drained. When Honorine suggested that he rest for a while, he offered no objection.

Watson retired to the sitting room and, remembering the way Lydie Denier had looked at him, pulled down a book from Verne's crammed shelves and set about reading the French text in order to improve his fluency of the language.

But it was no good. He simply couldn't concentrate. Even when he managed to forget about Lydie, which was not easy, there was too much else going on just now. Verne had made a good point earlier. How were they going to smuggle Gaston out of the city without anyone following them? Verne himself seemed to have set much store by the man Felix Nadar, but Watson preferred to reserve judgement.

Then there was Holmes. He had no idea when his friend was coming back, but it certainly wouldn't be before tomorrow.

Tomorrow, he thought. *With any luck Gaston will be out of the city by tomorrow, which will mean one less problem to worry about.* And tomorrow afternoon, he and Verne would be entertaining Lydie.

Lydie, he thought. What a romantic fool he was to be thinking so much about a woman he knew nothing about and had only just met.

*

Sometime after four o'clock the doorbell rang. Watson jumped up and reached into his pocket for his service revolver. A few moments later the maid showed Verne's doctor, Simonet, into the room.

'I have made all the necessary arrangements,' he reported. 'They are expecting Gaston at the Valois Institute, near Le Combeau, where he will be admitted under the name Paul Leveque. It was the safest place I could think of, and *le directeur* is a personal friend of mine.'

'Thank you, Doctor. One day you may understand just how vital your assistance has been.'

Verne came down to supper at about six. Neither he nor Watson had much appetite. Watson passed along Dr Simonet's message and Verne nodded in satisfaction.

'Le Combeau ... it is a good way from here, seven, eight hundred kilometres. Safe enough, I hope.'

After the meal Verne disappeared to consult his maps of the area. Watson, feeling he should try to get some sleep in order to be as fresh as possible for the events of the coming night, went to his room. At first sleep eluded him. This business had wound him too tight. But somewhere along the way he must have dozed off, for when he woke again it was dark.

He sat up and tilted his pocket watch to the meagre light filtering through the window. It was almost half past eight. He sighed. He still had the better part of three hours to kill.

He went to the chamber-set on the lowboy and splashed his face with cold water. Immediately he felt somewhat revived. But as he finished drying himself off, he thought he heard a soft but distinctive scratch of sound through the partly open window. He froze.

Someone had just opened the gate leading into the Verne courtyard.

He quickly stepped to one side of the window and

cautiously peered down through the breeze-blown lace. At first he saw no one. Then he stiffened. *There!* A figure was loitering in the shadows beside the gate, staring up at the house.

Watson wondered what he should do. He did not think the newcomer could possibly be a visitor. No visitor would linger there in the darkness, just watching the house. Nor would he make his entrance in such a secretive manner.

Then the figure broke away from the wall and crossed the courtyard smoothly and silently, following his moon-thrown shadow ever closer.

Whoever he was, Watson decided that he was up to no good.

He quickly slipped into his jacket. The weight of his revolver in the right-side pocket was a comfort. Leaving his room, he descended the stairs. Not wanting to alarm the Vernes unduly, he moved silently past the sitting room until he reached the deserted kitchen, where he carefully unbolted the back door.

Outside the night was sharp and cold, the sky clear and glittering with stars. The steady breeze tightened his skin. He closed the door softly behind him and then, keeping his back to the wall, edged along the side of the house until he reached the corner turning into the courtyard.

It took a moment before he spotted the intruder. He was standing in the middle of the courtyard, looking up at the house.

Watson wondered who he was and what he was planning to do. Simultaneously it came to him that perhaps this man had already done what he'd come for. Someone wanted Verne dead. Was it possible that this man had set a bomb on the steps and was just taking one last look to make sure that everything was as it should be with his handiwork?

The idea alarmed Watson. Throwing caution to the wind he broke cover and, as fast as his limp would allow, charged across the lawn. His target – a man in a long grey overcoat and tall hat – wheeled around to face him, eyes bulging with shock.

In the next moment Watson threw himself at the intruder and they went down in a tangle of arms and legs. Grappling on the ground, they rolled uncaring through the flowerbeds, crushing gerberas, lilies and daffodils as they went.

Finally Watson managed to grab his opponent by the shoulders and, rising, hoisted him to his feet. Light from the street revealed a long face topped by a wild shock of brown hair. The intruder was in his twenties, his features – a sloping brow, a long, straight nose – typically Gallic.

Watson drew back his fist, but the other man struck first. He hit Watson on the jaw. Watson staggered backwards, shaking his head as if, in the process, he might also shake loose the pain. Regaining his balance, he prepared to meet the charge he expected to follow. But the man was busily shaking his right hand, the expression of pain on his face the very match of Watson's own.

Stupidly, Watson felt a wholly irrational stab of pride; that even in the act of taking a punch he had been able to inflict pain upon his opponent.

A moment later someone raised the gas in the conservatory hall and a shaft of smoky light spilled out across the courtyard. Verne's manservant came outside, yelling: 'You there! Who are you? What do you think you're doing?'

Watson and the other man both spun towards him as the manservant drew up short, his face wide with surprise. 'Docteur Watson!' he exclaimed. And then: 'M'sieur Verne?'

Watson frowned. *Verne?*

The other man bent down and retrieved his fallen hat. *'Oui,'* he said, glaring at Watson. 'I wasn't sure of the reception I would get when I finally came to visit my father, but I never expected this!'

As the combatants turned again to face each other, Watson said sheepishly: 'You are Michel Verne?'

Michel nodded. His tired smile resembled a grimace. 'And you, *m'sieur*...?'

'My name is Watson. I have been staying here as your father's—'

'—bodyguard?' the younger man said sourly.

'—guest,' finished Watson. 'I saw you – someone – skulking around in the courtyard and, well, with everything that has happened over the last few days—'

'It is all right, *m'sieur*,' Michel said wearily. 'I can see how it must have looked. To be candid with you, I have been debating whether or not to come ever since I heard the news that my father had been shot. Shot! And by his dreamy little mouse, at that. But as you may or may not know, my father and I have been … at odds … for some time now. He considers me a profligate and a wastrel, and in all honesty I cannot say he is entirely mistaken. But blood is blood, M'sieur Watson—'

'It's doctor, actually.'

'*Docteur*,' Michel continued with a nod of acknowledgement, 'and for all his faults, he is the only father I have. I came hoping to make my peace with him, but even as my courage deserted me upon seeing the house again after so long, so did nostalgia replace it. I stood there, wondering why things could not have been different, and was about to leave when—'

Watson studied the other. Inasmuch as he had expected anything at all, he had expected someone much different to this man. The son Jules Verne had told him about had sounded like a callous, selfish cad. This man seemed genuinely sorry for the behaviour of his earlier years.

'I can only apologize,' Watson murmured. 'I had the welfare of your parents at heart.'

'And for that I am grateful, *Docteur*. Tell me – I have read of the incident in the papers. My God, they are full of it! But how has the incident really affected him?'

Watson shrugged. 'The physical injury itself will heal, though he will limp for the rest of his days. As for the emotional damage … it is hard to say. My understanding is that he and Gaston enjoyed a cordial relationship. The fact that it was Gaston who made the attempt upon his life … well, it has obviously affected him.'

'Gaston …' Michel said contemptuously.

Watson studied him briefly, then said: 'Are you ready to go inside?'

Michel offered a rueful smile. '*Oui, m'sieur.* Let us get it over with.'

Together they crossed the yard and entered the house. Verne and Honorine were waiting for them in the hallway. There was a moment of silence as father and son looked at each other. Watson, staying well in the background, could only guess at their thoughts – that each was perhaps shocked by just how much older the other looked, that neither had ever really expected this moment of reunion to come.

Then Michel swallowed and said formally: 'Mama … Papa.'

As Verne stared at his son, tears moistened his eyes. He opened his mouth to speak, but no words came out. After another moment he seemed to remember where he was, and offered his hand, saying: 'Michel….'

Michel took his father's hand, the muscles of his face twitching with emotion. 'Papa! It is good to see you again. When I heard you had been shot—'

'What brings you here at this hour, Michel?' Verne interrupted.

Michel stepped back a little, shocked by the iciness in his father's tone. 'An epiphany, if you like,' he replied mildly. 'A moment of absolute clarity in which everything that was previously hidden became as clear as day to me. I came to apologize for my past behaviour, to apologize for bringing shame upon you and upon the family name. I came to make my peace … if you will accept it.'

Verne shook his head, clearly bewildered. 'I don't know what to say …' he managed, clearing his throat. 'For so many years we have been at loggerheads, you and I. You have rejected everything I have ever done to help you—'

'And for that you must blame the impetuosity of youth,' Michel said with feeling. 'I understand that this cannot be easy for you. I have thought only of myself for far too long, and in so doing hurt you both. But perhaps some good has come of Gaston's madness. Had you died, I would forever have been denied the chance to tell you how sorry I am. If truth be told, I am not sure I could have lived much longer with that upon my conscience. And so I am here now, in hope of reconciliation. But I understand your scepticism. I have been every dark thing you have ever called me. But I am an older and wiser man now, with a child of my own – your grandchild, Papa, a fine boy. All I ask is the chance to prove myself.'

It was more than Verne could take. Relenting, his face reflecting his joy, he drew Michel to him and buried his face in the young man's shoulder. Watson watched Verne's hands as he clung to his son, the way his long fingers tightened as if he couldn't hold him close enough. Only once did he sob. Otherwise, he cried in silence.

When father and son finally broke apart, Michel pulled a handkerchief from his pocket, wiped his eyes and blew his nose. 'From this moment, Papa, I am your servant. Ask of me what you will. I shall never let you down again.'

Emotion had drained Verne, and his wife had to help him to a chair. 'I never thought to see this day,' he said thickly. 'You have your chance, Michel. In fact, you may have your chance this very night.'

Michel cocked his head questioningly. 'Papa?'

Before answering, Verne looked at Watson, who had himself been affected by the reunion between the two. Watson nodded for Verne to go ahead. Verne turned back to Michel, saying: 'I am going to tell you as much as I know about this wretched business, my son, and rely upon you to let it go no further. And when I am finished, I am going to ask your help in a very delicate matter.'

'To do what, Papa?'

'Help us get Gaston out of Amiens,' Verne said. 'At midnight.'

CHAPTER TWENTY-ONE

The Giant

As Verne's carriage rattled through the dark, sleeping streets, Watson said: 'Are you *sure* you're up to this, sir? Michel and I are perfectly capable of handling the matter.'

'He is right, Papa,' Michel chimed in. 'You have been through enough already. There is nothing to be gained by putting yourself through yet more.'

'No,' Verne said determinedly. 'Though I am not entirely responsible for Gaston's madness, I have played a generous part in it. I cannot shirk my duty now. Besides—' He smiled briefly '—I have two stout fellows to help me.'

In the darkness Watson saw Michel reach impulsively for his father's hand and fondly squeeze it.

At last they reached Rue de la Republique. Inspector Mathes was standing on the steps in front of the police station, smoking a cigarette. Watson climbed out into the quiet street and made a slow, careful examination of their surroundings.

Mathes said quietly: 'Rest easy, *Docteur.* I have been watching for the past twenty minutes. The shadows are empty.'

'Is Gaston ready?'

'I shall fetch him. Have your coach back up to the mouth of that alley.'

As the inspector ground his cigarette underfoot and entered the building, Watson conveyed instructions to the driver. Michel had also alighted, and was keeping a watchful eye on street.

Shortly Mathes appeared out of the shadows, leading
Gaston by the arm. Gaston stumbled along meekly, a young
man lost in his own world. Michel stared at him, barely able to
believe the change in his cousin. Gaston had always been a
loner, certainly, but he had always possessed vitality and a
constant and seemingly unquenchable thirst for discovery.
Now he hardly seemed aware of anything.

Michel stepped forward and took him gently by the other
arm. Then, while Watson shook hands with Mathes and
thanked him for his assistance, Michel helped Gaston to climb
into the carriage. Verne, hunched in the corner, caught a
glimpse of his nephew in the streetlamps. Something tugged
at his heart and he quickly rubbed his watery eyes on his
sleeve.

Michel followed Gaston into the carriage. It rocked gently as
he helped Gaston get comfortable. Then Watson climbed in,
closed the door and tapped on the roof with his cane. The
driver snapped the reins and the carriage jolted back into
motion.

'Where are we going now?' Watson asked Verne.

'Somewhere far from prying eyes.'

'And your friend, Nadar…?'

'He will be there,' said Verne.

'Are you not familiar with Felix Nadar, *Docteur*?' asked
Michel.

'No.'

'Amazing,' Michel said. 'He is so well known in this country
that you could write his name alone on an envelope and guarantee that the letter would reach him. He has worked as a
drama critic, a shop clerk, a caricature artist, a pamphleteer –
you name it, he has done it. You and he even co-founded The
Society for the Encouragement of Aerial Locomotion by Means
of Heavier than Air Machines, didn't you, Papa?'

Verne nodded. 'Yes. He was president, I was secretary. A
remarkable man, and one we may trust implicitly with the

task ahead. This entire business has taken nerve, *Docteur*, more nerve than I thought I possessed. But Felix ... ah, now there is a man who thrives upon this kind of danger. He has photographed the stinking Paris sewers and taken his camera into a hot-air balloon to photograph the Arc de Triomphe from above. He is our man, right enough, and one's life is always the richer for having made his acquaintance.'

A brisk twenty-minute drive took them into the heart of the surrounding countryside. Moonlight showed Watson endless, sloping fields of wheat and lavender. There was an onion field close by; he could smell it. At last the coach drew to a halt and Verne gestured that they had reached their destination.

Watson climbed out. The night was still and colder than ever. Off to the west he saw a scattering of dwellings on the slope of a plateau and wondered aloud what the name of the place was.

'Saveuse,' Verne said, struggling to get comfortable on his crutches. 'It is little more than a hamlet, and filled with country folk who retire early to their beds.'

To the south and east Watson could just make out the undulating silhouette of a dense forest. 'You have certainly chosen your spot well,' he confessed. 'But I see no sign of M'sieur Nadar.'

'He will be here,' Verne said confidently.

He and his son shared a knowing smile.

Watson glanced into the carriage. Gaston sat there listlessly, head tilted to one side. A sound in the nearby hedge startled Watson and he quickly turned around.

'It is all right, my friend,' Verne cautioned. 'The countryside hereabout teems with life – everything from red deer and ibex to foxes and mountain hares.'

They continued to wait. Bats fluttered overhead. Suddenly Michel stiffened and whispered: 'I see him.'

Watson peered in the direction Michel indicated. 'Good grief!' he gasped.

A hot-air balloon was slowly drifting in from the south, a large woven wicker basket swaying gently beneath it. Every so often the pilot – presumably Felix Nadar – opened the propane valve above his head to send a great spear of flame up into the balloon. Even from this distance they could hear the brief accompanying roar.

'Metier,' said Verne.

At his order the coach driver lit a crude torch and, standing up in the high seat, waved it slowly above his head.

A few seconds later the balloon began to descend until its pilot found the right current of air to propel him in their direction.

Watson took a long, fascinated look at the craft. The balloon itself was the shape of an upside-down onion, constructed of long, dark panels of fabric, below which was some kind of skirt. He smiled to himself. 'I can see now,' he said in admiration, 'how we may transport Gaston away from here without fear of anyone following him.'

Verne nodded. 'Many years ago, *Docteur,* Felix had an enormous balloon built. For obvious reasons it was called *Le Géant.* Its cab was two storeys high and it could carry fourteen people. But the flight ended badly, and both Felix and his wife were injured. As you can see, he has since opted for something smaller than *Le Géant.*'

'Yes. And he certainly knows how to—' He broke off suddenly.

'Yes, *Docteur?*'

Watson grinned at him. 'I believe I have just found the significance in your telegram, sir. *"Six-Quatre."* You refer of course to the Book of Genesis, Chapter Six, Verse Four – "There were giants in the earth in those days".'

Verne nodded and clapped him on the arm. 'Of course. Now, if you would be so kind as to help Gaston from the carriage?'

The balloon continued to descend smoothly towards a spot in the centre of the field before them. As Watson gently coaxed

Gaston out into the narrow lane he glanced over his shoulder and saw the pilot busily pulling cords to control his landing.

In their traces the horses whinnied and stamped, unnerved by the appearance and proximity of the balloon. Metier, the driver, muttered soothing words to calm them. He broke off suddenly.

"Yes, *m'sieur.*"

As the balloon set down, crushing wheat beneath it, Verne said: '*Venez.*'

With Michel helping him, he used his crutches to swing himself forward through the wheat rows. Watson followed with Gaston stumbling blankly along beside him.

Having secured his balloon by means of an anchor, Felix Nadar scrambled out of the basket and hurried to meet them. To Watson's surprise he was quite elderly – well into his sixties. Of average height and somewhat overweight, he had dark, lively eyes in a round face. His unruly hair was receding and hung down over his collar.

He and Verne hugged and fondly clapped each other on the back. Then Verne introduced his companions. Nadar was warm and affable, a man who took great joy in every aspect of life, and whose joy was curiously contagious.

'This is quite the adventure, eh?' he enthused.

'Something like that, sir,' Watson replied, taking another look around to make sure they hadn't been followed.

'I have the co-ordinates here for your destination in Le Combeau,' said Verne. 'Once there, Michel will see that Gaston is safely installed at the hospital and will make his own way back to Amiens by train.'

'Very well,' said Nadar, looking at the scrap of paper Verne had handed him. 'We will have the young man under medical care by dawn.'

'*Merçi,* Felix. You are a good friend.'

'Then I am to you what you are to me.'

They shook hands, and then Verne turned to Gaston. Moonlight showed Watson the pain Verne felt at seeing his nephew's true condition.

'My poor dreamy mouse,' Verne whispered. 'I am so sorry it had to come to this.'

He hugged Gaston, kissed him on both cheeks and allowed Michel and Nadar to lead him away. Verne then turned to Watson. 'Please forgive a foolish old man his tears, *Docteur.*'

'There is nothing to forgive.'

They stood side by side, watching as Gaston was lifted into the basket. Michel clambered in behind him. Nadar waved, then hauled in the anchor and busied himself at his propane valve. A jet of amber flame stabbed up into the balloon, blasting a harsh snarl out across the empty countryside. The balloon slowly began to rise. A moment later the basket left the ground, swaying sluggishly back and forth ... and Gaston was on his way.

Watson and Verne watched until the balloon was almost out of sight. Then Verne gave a satisfied nod and sighed as if a great weight had been lifted from his shoulders. 'Now,' he said quietly, 'let us return to Amiens – and whatever fate awaits us.'

CHAPTER TWENTY-TWO

A Guiding Light

Dr Edouard Orand gestured for Holmes to take a seat on the visitor's side of his desk. As director of the Sanatorium de Russy, located just outside Blois, he was a meticulous, prissy disciplinarian who enjoyed his authority to the full. 'You will forgive me if I cannot give you as much time as perhaps you would like,' he said with as much criticism as he felt he could get away with. 'But had you given me even the briefest notice of your visit—'

Holmes cut him off. 'I apologize for the oversight,' he replied easily. 'But the journey from Nantes took three hours, and my schedule is such that, by the time I arrived in Blois, the opportunity to wire ahead did not present itself.'

'Naturally,' said Orand. He was an odd-looking little man. Though well into his forties, he was about the size of a fifteen-year-old boy. He had a thin, sallow face and cold, toffee-coloured eyes that were magnified to almost comical proportions by the thick lenses in his wire-framed spectacles. Beneath his long white coat he wore a creased grey suit, and gave by his every movement an impression of nervous energy. Every time he fidgeted, his dark, shield-shaped tie pin reflected the light of the new day.

'Now,' he continued, 'I know you are here to ask about the recent, unfortunate escape of Gaston Verne – the letter of introduction written by his father tells me as much – but how exactly can I help you, *m'sieur*?'

'Firstly, may I enquire as to your diagnosis of Gaston Verne?'

Without a word Orand rose and went to a wooden file cabinet. While he unlocked it and then riffled through its contents, Holmes turned to the window and surveyed the ominous oaks of the Forêt de Russy beyond the grounds. The fact that they formed a natural barrier to the outside world was not lost upon him. Not only did they keep out prying eyes, they also lent a grim remoteness to the sanatorium.

Orand now brought a file back to his desk. He opened it, scanned it briefly and said: 'The patient was admitted some months ago upon the advice of his own family doctor, who diagnosed mania, melancholia, extreme neurasthenia and hysteria, the latter condition being unusual in that it is more closely associated with the fairer sex. He had a dull aspect and a sulky nature, paid little attention to what was said to him, but was frequently prone to sleeplessness, unmanageable conduct, violent language and acts. He tore his clothing, bit himself, broke windows, showed immoderate laughter for no apparent cause and chattered to imaginary people and things.

'Upon those occasions when he was questioned he answered in an abhorrently ill-tempered tone. There was no evidence of bodily disease and no evidence of injury to the head. For this and other reasons, it quickly became obvious to my colleagues and I that his condition was incurable, but quite possibly controllable. We were experimenting with various chemical and homeopathic methods to find the most beneficial one when he … escaped.'

'What methods?'

'In the initial stages of his stay he was considered as much a risk to himself as to those around him. Therefore we used opiates to make him more … compliant.'

'And how did he escape?'

'As near as we have been able to discover, he somehow secreted a dinner knife about his person and upon the night he vanished used it to force open the lock to his room.'

Holmes's eyebrows arched in a mixture of surprise.

'Is there something wrong, *m'sieur?*' asked Orand.

'Only that I find that a remarkable achievement for one who was at the time undergoing a powerful drug treatment to control his actions.'

Orand's lips thinned. 'You must forgive me, M'sieur Holmes, but I don't quite know what you are implying.'

'I'm not *implying* anything,' Holmes said. 'I'm merely making an observation.' Then, firing the question like a bullet: 'Where was Gaston's room?'

'On the first floor.'

'So he escaped from his room, made his way along a corridor to the staircase, descended the stairs to…?'

'The door leading from the kitchen to the back yard.'

'And disappeared into the forest?'

'That was the finding of our subsequent investigation.'

'You have staff who patrol your wards at night, do you not?'

'Of course.'

'And yet Gaston managed to avoid them all.'

Orand closed the file with a snap. '*M'sieur*, I do not appreciate your accusatory tone. But to answer your question: the night of March second was especially hectic for us. There was a full moon and for reasons we still do not fully comprehend, the full moon exerts a detrimental effect upon the majority of our patients. It makes them restive and troublesome. My staff were kept fully occupied in other parts of the building – a fortunate happenstance for Gaston.'

'Fortunate indeed,' said Holmes. 'But I am afraid inaccurate, Doctor.'

'I beg your pardon?'

'The last full moon occurred on February eighteenth. The next will occur on March twentieth. The night Gaston Verne escaped there was but a crescent moon, it being three days before the appearance of the new one.'

'I trust you are not calling me a liar, sir?' Orand said, flustered.

'I am merely stating a fact, Docteur Orand.'

'Well, be that as it may, the *fact* remains that it was a particularly troublesome night, and my staff could not be everywhere at once.'

'May I see Gaston's room?'

'Do you think it will help?'

'It can do no harm, surely?'

'No, but you will appreciate that I am anxious to avoid anything that could possibly embarrass the sanatorium.'

'I have no interest in making things difficult for you, *Docteur*.'

'Very well. I will have one of the warders accompany you to the first floor.'

A few minutes later a tall, thick-set warder led Holmes along the first-floor corridor, his pace brisk and businesslike, his steps and those of Holmes clattering back at them from off the black and white tiled floor. Eventually the warder came to a halt before the room Gaston had occupied during his stay. The warder, who had introduced himself as Widmeyer, unlocked the door, pushed it open and told Holmes that he was free to go inside and look around.

Holmes did so. The room was small and sparsely furnished. He checked the lowboy. The drawers were empty. He went back to the door, knelt and inspected the areas between the door frame and the lock for any suspicious scrapes or marks. As he had suspected, there were none. A knife could indeed be used to open a door by the simple means of pushing the lock back from its seat, but it was useless on a locked door.

As Widmeyer watched, Holmes took a small tool case from his pocket, unclipped it and rolled it out on the floor. He selected a screwdriver and went to work, unscrewing the plate over the lock. When he had removed it he carefully blew away any dust and with a magnifying glass inspected the pins for dents and scratches. Again, there was no evidence that the lock had been tampered with.

'Strange, isn't it, *m'sieur*,' Widmeyer said.

Holmes looked up at him. 'What is?'

'Strange that M'sieur Gaston should take it into his head to escape on one of the coldest nights of the year and leave his every stitch of clothing behind.'

Frowning, Holmes straightened up again. 'You know this for a fact?'

Widmeyer nodded gravely. He was a brawny, uncouth-looking man with surprisingly compassionate green eyes. 'I was one of the men who cleaned the room out after he vanished, sir,' he said quietly.

Glancing around to make sure they wouldn't be overheard, he entered the room and closed the door behind him. 'I liked M'sieur Gaston,' he said. 'He was a handful when he first came here, but after a while the medication seemed to calm him down, and when he was calm he was no trouble to anyone. I feel I can tell you this because Docteur Orand said you were here at the request of M'sieur Gaston's father.'

'Tell me what?'

'That there is something amiss here, sir.'

Holmes put the magnifying glass back into his pocket. 'You are quite sure about his clothing?'

'As sure as I can be, sir. He did not have many things here. Very few of the patients do. There is no need. I am almost prepared to swear that he took nothing with him but the nightshirt he was wearing at the time, sir. Besides....'

'Go on,' Holmes said. 'You may speak freely, Widmeyer. I shall not break your confidence.'

The warder looked uncomfortable, then took a deep breath before saying: 'There is a man here by the name of Bertrand Joncas. Kitchen staff, sir – and yet he was on duty the night M'sieur Gaston escaped. Killing cockroaches, they say. You know, they come out after dark, sir, and it's the best time to catch them.'

'And...?'

'Although he claimed to have seen nothing during the time M'sieur Gaston is said to have escaped, I noticed – I don't know, perhaps it was just me – but he seemed *nervous,* somehow. Edgy. At first I thought he might be worried for his job. You know, that Docteur Orand would use him as a scape-grace, make an example of him and dismiss him. But it did not come to that.'

'Why not?'

'Because Bertrand Joncas was killed less than thirty-six hours later, sir, stabbed in a back alley, the victim of a botched robbery, they said.'

'The police, you mean?'

'*Oui, m'sieur.*'

'But you don't believe them?'

'Kitchen staff is paid even less than warders, *m'sieur.* Bertrand Joncas was a poor man, *always* poor. And a poor choice to be robbed.'

Holmes considered for a moment before saying: 'Are you suggesting there was another motive for his murder?'

'I'm suggesting there could well be. If he was paid to turn a blind eye while M'sieur Gaston "escaped", perhaps he was silenced to make sure he didn't break and give anything away afterwards. In any case, there is something else.'

'Go on.'

'I was on duty the day M'sieur Gaston received a visitor. Docteur Orand had me show him up here just as he had me show you up here today.'

'Did he say who this man was?'

'*Non, m'sieur.* I had the impression he was a doctor who had come to assess M'sieur Gaston's condition for himself.'

'Did he stay long?'

'*Non, m'sieur.*'

'Did you hear anything of his conversation with Gaston?'

'*Non, m'sieur.*'

'You did not know this man?'

'I'd never seen him before.'

'What did he look like?'

'Tall, thin, perhaps fifty.'

'Colouring?'

'His hair was silver and he wore a chin-beard. I didn't really think too much about him at the time. It was only after M'sieur Gaston vanished that I wondered if he had said something that put the idea of escape into Gaston's mind, or that he himself had in some way arranged the entire business.'

'What makes you say that?'

Widmeyer shrugged. '*Je ne sais quoi.* Perhaps I am just seeing things that aren't really there. Perhaps I should be one of the patients instead of one of the warders, eh? But this man, he wore a very distinctive tie pin. I remembered it because the superintendent often wears one just like it.'

Holmes frowned. 'Is he wearing it today?'

'*Oui, m'sieur.* A small black shield bearing three small clusters of grapes, and the letters *X* and *I*.'

'I noticed it, also,' Holmes said thoughtfully.

Widmeyer shifted uncomfortably from one foot to the other. 'Begging your pardon, *m'sieur*, but do you think I have too much imagination?'

'On the contrary,' said Holmes. 'I believe you have been a great help in my investigation. A true guiding light, in fact.'

CHAPTER TWENTY-THREE

Family Reunion

By the time Holmes returned to the room he had rented at a local hotel in Blois, night was already blackening the sky. Upon his return from the sanatorium he had visited the local library and spent the remainder of the afternoon poring over books with almost obsessive zeal. Indeed, he would have continued his research well into the night had the library not closed at six o'clock. But, forced to leave, he stopped at a café and ordered a lemon pressé and a bowl of soup.

Later, deep in thought, he wandered the steep, winding streets of Blois for a time, mulling over what he had learned and trying to make sense of it all. He walked until he was weary and then headed back to his hotel. Tomorrow, he promised himself, he would return to Amiens and make another attempt to convince Verne to confess what he knew.

As soon as let himself into his darkened room, he knew he was not alone. But he felt no fear. Indeed, he allowed himself a rare smile.

'Mycroft,' he said. 'How good of you to make yourself at home.'

A deep, curmudgeonly voice from the darkness on the other side of the room said: 'I should have known. It was the polish, wasn't it?'

'Of course.'

Holmes struck a match, raised the gas and turned to the corpulent figure of his brother, who was sprawled in a corner armchair. 'The Diogenes Club, that fusty residence wherein members treasure their solitude and may not under any circumstances address or even acknowledge the presence of their fellow misanthropes upon penalty of expulsion, has a distinct aroma of Brazil wax and beeswax. If one spends precisely two hours and fifty-five minutes there every day, as you do, dear brother, it is inevitable that your clothes will eventually absorb so much of the odour that even the best dry cleaners in London cannot entirely erase it.'

Mycroft Holmes gave a hearty laugh. They were as chalk is to cheese, these two. Though they shared the same distinctive, deep-set grey eyes, Mycroft was massive in build and irredeemably lazy. His mind, however, was razor-sharp; sharper even than that of his more famous younger brother. He was, in Holmes's own words, a human fount of knowledge. He worked for the British government in some powerful but never clearly defined position. His job, as near as Holmes had ever been able to understand, was simply to process the conclusions of every department in Whitehall and see patterns therein that eluded all others. Mycroft's stock-in-trade was omniscience.

'And how did you know where to find me?' Holmes asked, sitting on the edge of the single bed.

'I *always* know where to find you, brother. Surely by now you must know that.'

'And your purpose here now is ... what, exactly?'

'To warn you,' Mycroft said, his affable manner suddenly vanishing. 'You are involved in something much, much larger than you know.'

'The Knaves, you mean?'

Mycroft raised one eyebrow in admiration. 'You have truly surpassed yourself, Sherlock. Few indeed even know of their existence. How did you come to that conclusion?'

'I have spent a most profitable afternoon studying heraldry. It was a time-consuming business, but it has paid handsome dividends. I have identified the group behind the attempt to kill Jules Verne.'

'There was more to it than that, surely?'

'Last week a man came to visit Gaston Verne shortly before his alleged "escape" from the Sanatorium de Russy. He wore a black tie pin which depicted three separate clusters of grapes set out in triangular formation, over the letters *X* and *I*. I could not find any such symbol in the books I consulted, but I did find a remarkable resemblance within the family crest of Etienne de Vignolles.' He eyed his brother askance. 'You are familiar with the name, of course?'

'Naturally. De Vignolles fought alongside Jean d'Arc in the Hundred Years' War.'

'Then you will also know that he is commemorated as the face of *La Hire,* in a deck of playing cards. *La Hire* – The Knave.'

'That is all very interesting, but what of the letters *X* and *I*?'

'Roman numerals, brother,' said Holmes. 'As if you didn't know. They represent the number eleven – the jack, or knave's, position within the deck, coming as it does just after the ten and just before the queen.'

'You seem remarkably sure of your deduction.'

'I am. I did not get much from questioning Gaston Verne, but I did get a set of initials, "V.D.C.". They of course stand for *valet de cœur* – the knave of hearts.'

'And who *is* this group?'

'I fancy you know rather more about that than I. But I would imagine they have their collective fingers in France's political pie, otherwise they would not have attracted your particular interest.'

Mycroft slowly shifted his bulky body to a more comfortable position. 'There is something remarkably curious about the otherwise unremarkable knave,' he said. 'In recent years he has grown from the lowest of all the court figures to oft-times the highest position in the rank of cards. What does that imply to you, brother?'

'That he is the power behind the throne,' Holmes said.

'Exactly! In this instance, the Knaves associate most closely with the Independent Republicans, but they have their own agenda. Look closely and you will find that it is they who are orchestrating this campaign to oust Prime Minister de Freycinet. They want to put their own man in, and like the puppet masters they are, run everything from the shadows, invisibly.'

Holmes frowned. 'If you already know this, why not take your findings to the French government?'

'Because we have no real way of knowing who can be trusted.' Mycroft's fleshy lips tightened sardonically. 'Naturally, it is in our interest, and the interests of those in the rest of Europe, to have the right people running the country. Get the wrong man at the helm and it could affect politics, trade, whole economies.'

'But what has this to do with Verne?'

'My dear brother, I believe you well know the answer to that.'

Holmes could not deny it. 'You have not come to warn me off, then?'

'On the contrary, Sherlock, if you can destroy or otherwise bring about the destruction of this unholy group, you will be doing the free world a great service. I should have liked to remove them myself when they first began to assemble, but even one in my position is sometimes limited in what he can and cannot do. However, it is important for the people to make up their own minds as to who rules them. We can try to sway them with argument and debate, but when murder is employed, well, it just isn't the done thing.'

'I will do everything I can.'

'No one can expect more,' Mycroft said. 'All I ask is that you take care in the doing of it. I should hate to lose you just yet, dear brother – especially to a French assassin.'

CHAPTER TWENTY-FOUR

What is in a Man's Heart

Holmes caught the train back to Amiens the following afternoon. He would have returned earlier, but just before he left his hotel room for the last time he was once again racked by the symptoms of opiate withdrawal. This time the attack left him drained, and yet he sensed a curious finality to the experience that he had not felt on previous occasions. It also left him alternately shivering and sweating for a time, but he believed that he had finally seen the last of the after effects of his reckless cocaine binge.

As Blois fell behind him and the train click-clacked rhythmically over the rails bound for Amiens, he thought again about his unexpected meeting with Mycroft. The Knaves were powerful indeed if they had become a source of concern to that particular worthy. Mycroft was not merely a representative of Her Majesty's government; upon certain occasions he *was* the government. And Mycroft's instructions had been clear. He was to destroy the group in any way possible, so long as he didn't turn the matter into an embarrassing diplomatic incident.

He reached Amiens four hours later, still wondering how this could be accomplished. Only one thing was certain at present; he would have to choose his allies with care.

The façade of Gare du Nord had been plastered with yet more hastily pasted Independent Republican posters. Holmes paused momentarily to read some of them. It was Sunday afternoon, and the centre of Amiens was almost deserted.

Ten minutes later he arrived at Rue Charles Dubois and pulled the bell. It was answered in short order by Watson, who was delighted to see him back. 'Here, Holmes, let me take your bag.'

'Thank you. You received my wire, of course. I deduce from your attitude that you successfully managed to smuggle Gaston out of the city?'

'Holmes, you will never believe how we did it! We—'

They had just entered the hallway when Holmes suddenly raised one hand for silence. 'Where is Verne?' he snapped.

'In the sitting room.'

'Alone?'

'No, we have a visit–'

He got no further. All at once Holmes was a blur of motion as he raced to the sitting-room door and to Watson's complete surprise burst in unannounced.

Verne was seated on the chaise in the bay window, his left leg resting on a stool. An attractive young woman with dark hair was seated beside Honorine on the sofa a few feet away. Between them was a low table upon which sat a tray and various tea-things.

Both the Vernes and their visitor turned towards Holmes, startled by his unexpected entrance. 'M'sieur Holmes!' Verne himself exclaimed. 'What is the meaning of this interruption?'

'My apologies,' said Holmes. 'I did not mean to startle you.'

'Well, I am afraid you *did*,' murmured Honorine.

Ignoring the criticism in her tone, Holmes fixed his attention on their visitor. 'You must forgive me, *mademoiselle*, but I have a curious feeling we have met before.'

'I do not believe so,' she replied stiffly.

'This is Miss Lydie Denier,' said Verne, still clearly annoyed by Holmes's lapse in manners. 'She writes for *L'Amoureaux des Livres* and she is conducting an interview with me – or rather, *trying* to.'

'*L'Amoureaux des Livres?*' Holmes repeated, taking her hand by the fingertips and bowing his head. 'That would be a literary magazine?'

'Yes,' Lydie replied. She looked immaculate in a well-tailored, emerald-green basque and a matching skirt worn over a bustle.

'I believe I have heard of it,' said Holmes. 'The editor is Théophile Constantin, I believe.'

'*Non, m'sieur.* My editor's name is Emmanuel Jarnett.'

'Jarnett?' said Holmes with sudden interest. 'The poet?'

'He has written some poetry in the past,' Lydie said smoothly. 'And I suspect he would be flattered that you have heard of him. But these days his editorial responsibilities keep him too busy to write much of anything.'

'Such a shame. He has a most unusual approach to prosody, and rather refreshingly tries to avoid the iambic parameter at every opportunity.'

Lydie hesitated briefly before saying: 'I shall have to take your word for that, *m'sieur.* I have read his work, of course, but not made such a detailed study of it. I much prefer fiction.'

'Yes,' Holmes said. 'I imagine you do.'

In the uncomfortable silence that followed, she set her cup down and turned her attention back to Verne. 'Well, I believe I have taken up far more of your time than I should have, *m'sieur.*' Rising, she gathered her things together. 'You have been most accommodating, and I am grateful.'

Verne used his cane to help himself up. 'Must you go so soon, *mademoiselle*? I feel we have only just scratched the surface of our interview.'

'Perhaps I could return in a few days,' she suggested.

'Yes,' said Honorine. 'And if you are still here on the twentieth, why don't you come to the ball we're having at Versailles?'

'A ball at Versailles?' Lydie said, surprised. 'May I ask what the occasion is, *madame*?'

Honorine had been so distressed by all the turmoil

surrounding her husband since he had been shot that she immediately warmed to this much happier subject. 'Well, we usually throw parties here at the house every time Jules has a new book published. But this year we celebrate the thirtieth anniversary of our very first meeting. The thing has been in the planning forever, or so it seems. I would willingly cancel until Jules is fully recovered, but he won't hear of it.'

'*Jules*,' Verne reminded her with mock severity, 'is still in the room with you, so please stop talking about him as if he's not here!'

Honorine reached out and rubbed his hand affectionately. 'Forgive me, dearest.' She smiled at Watson, who had just discreetly entered the room. 'Believe me, Dr Watson and I are *very* much aware of your presence.'

Watson chuckled at her little joke and moved over behind Holmes.

'Seriously, *mademoiselle*,' Honorine continued to Lydie, 'we should be delighted if you will accept.'

'And I should be delighted if you will allow me to escort you,' Watson said impulsively.

Lydie smiled up at him. 'Then I simply cannot refuse. Thank you, *m'sieur, madame*.'

'Come,' said Honorine. 'We will collect your coat and I will arrange for our coachman to take you back to your hotel.'

As soon as Lydie had left the room, Verne's affable manner turned frosty. 'I trust you have a very good reason for bursting in the way you did, M'sieur Holmes?'

'I do indeed,' Holmes replied. 'Watson, why don't you "escort" Mademoiselle Denier back to her hotel? And have a care, old friend. She is not all she pretends to be.'

Watson blanched. '*What?* How can you say that? She is a journalist here from Paris—'

'—who works for a magazine that does not exist, and discusses the poetry of a writer who does not exist, and wears a most distinctive perfume.'

'What the devil does that mean?'

'It means that I first smelled it when you were attending to M'sieur Verne, directly after he was shot. That woman was in the crowd.'

'Of course she was. She has made no secret of the fact. She was on her way here to request an interview with M'sieur Verne when Gaston shot him. The thing practically happened right under her nose.'

'I smelled the same perfume the night Gabriel Bessette tried to murder Gaston,' Holmes said. 'She was hiding in the shadows across the street from the police station, waiting to see whether or not Bessette's mission was successful.'

'Did you see her there?'

'I saw a woman, and I smelled that perfume.'

'Then I suggest you have been duped by an innocent coincidence and, as a result, have leapt to an erroneous conclusion.'

'On the contrary. It was you who first brought up the subject of Occam's Razor, Watson. The simplest explanation is usually the correct one.'

'Regardless, you are completely wrong about this woman.'

'Why? Because you have an eye for the fairer sex, and she is the fairest of them all?'

Watson reddened and spoke through gritted teeth. 'I think I deserve better than that from you.'

Holmes relented. 'You do indeed, and I apologize. But still, I need to know where I may find her again. The name of her hotel, and her room number.'

'Holmes, really—'

The door opened again and Lydie came in, wrapped in a double-breasted grey woollen coat, to say her goodbyes. Forcing himself to calm down, Watson said pleasantly: 'Come along, *mademoiselle*. If you have no objections, I shall see you safely back to your hotel.'

'I should appreciate the company,' she replied.

When they were gone, Holmes turned to Honorine and said:

'If I may, *madame,* I would like a few words with your husband alone.'

She looked at Verne, who appeared equally puzzled. Still, he nodded and Honorine withdrew. The door closed behind her and Verne studied Holmes for several long moments before saying: 'What have you discovered, *m'sieur*? You have discovered something. That much is obvious.'

Holmes said: 'Are you by any chance acquainted with François Fournier?'

'Fournier? Of course. He is the man the Independent Republicans are trying to make our next prime minister.'

'But do you know him ... personally.'

'I *used* to know him,' Verne admitted, almost reluctantly. 'He is a contemporary of my son's. They met at school, and it was through Michel that I was first introduced to him.'

'And from that introduction a friendship developed.'

'You could say that. Fournier was audacious, quick-witted, a good fellow. He was interested in politics even then, and had interesting ideas about how political life should be conducted. He always said he would choose diplomacy over force every time, that he was glad he possessed what he called the common touch, because that would encourage voters to trust him. Of course, he was always something of a mess; highly intelligent, but so reluctant to waste good time studying that he always found himself in the last quarter of his form. And yet he was also possessed of a remarkable memory, quick understanding and an enviable ability to apply himself when he had to. When he put his mind to it, he could outstrip the rest of his schoolmates with the least apparent effort.'

'And you found that an attractive attribute?'

'It is no secret that I was at that time somewhat ... disillusioned ... with my own son. During your absence, I am pleased to say that that situation has been resolved most satisfactorily. But at the time, Michel was as a stranger to me. In my desire to enjoy a father-son relationship ... yes, I did develop a certain affection for Fournier.'

'Did it ever become something more than that?'

Verne paled. 'I do not care for your insinuation, M'sieur Holmes. Indeed, I find it most repellent.'

'For that I apologize, M'sieur Verne. But I must press you for an honest answer.'

'You are asking if my relationship with Fournier was in any way ... unnatural?'

'That word, sir, is yours. Many would argue that love is a wholly *natural* emotion.'

'Even when it flourishes between a man and a boy?'

Silence filled the room.

'Were you lovers, sir?' asked Holmes.

Verne sat forward, inhaled noisily through his nose and angrily shook his head. 'You British,' he said scathingly. 'You have convinced yourselves that illness stems from the corruption of the spirit, and so you have adopted a sense of morality that is unworkable to keep that spirit as clean as it can be.'

'This is not about morality, sir,' said Holmes. 'I do not presume to judge you or anyone. But if I am to deal successfully with the problem facing us, I need honesty.' He came closer. 'Now, sir, since you are so reluctant to tell me the truth, I will tell you the facts of the business as I see them.

'There exists within this country a highly sophisticated network of businessmen who have formed and financed the Independent Republicans for one purpose only – to take control of this country. By your own admission, in François Fournier they have chosen a highly charismatic candidate for prime minister. But these are cautious men, M'sieur Verne. They have to be cautious, for there is much at stake, and everything to play for. They cannot afford to promote a candidate whose character is anything less than flawless.

'I believe that when they first approached Fournier they questioned him about his past ... indiscretions ... and your

name was mentioned. This organization – they call themselves
the Knaves, incidentally – immediately took steps to forestall
any potential embarrassment you may through accident or
design cause Fournier when he comes to power. They stole
Gaston away from the sanatorium with but one purpose – to
use him to kill you. So I ask you again, sir – was your relationship with Fournier ... questionable?'

Verne stared down at the carpet. He said something that
Holmes was unable to hear.

'What was that, sir?'

Verne looked up. 'I said a man cannot help what is in his
heart,' he repeated in a voice thick with shame. 'My relationship with Fournier did not start that way. I am not some
sick-minded individual who set out to seduce a minor. I
believed ... I *still* believe ... that my ... attraction, admiration,
call it what you will ... for young men stems from my desire to
be a father the way I wish I could have been a father to Michel.
Inevitably a certain ... fondness ... develops between like-
minded souls, regardless of their sex.'

'As it also developed with Gaston.'

'Yes,' said Verne, suddenly a much older man. 'He and I ...
we were so much alike. It was not difficult for me to love him
more than I should have.'

'And when your brother sensed that you were becoming too
close, and asked you to withdraw from your relationship with
Gaston—'

'It broke the poor boy's heart and caused him to have a
nervous breakdown.'

'Did your wife know the truth of this ... relationship?'

'No. But she is an intelligent woman. I believe she had her
suspicions.'

'I believe you are right, sir. She does not appear to have
much time for Gaston.' Holmes fell silent momentarily, then
said: 'Somehow the Knaves deduced the truth of the matter,
too, and decided that Gaston was the ideal candidate to

murder you. These are heartless men, sir. They must be stopped.'

'Even at the ruination of my good name?'

'It may not come to that,' said Holmes. 'Indeed, I will do everything within my power to ensure that the truth of the matter never comes out.'

Tears sprang to Verne's eyes. 'Thank you for that. But you are wrong about Fournier. I am sure of it! He was always a man of honour, and he would never do anything to harm his beloved France.'

'There is one way to find out.'

Verne frowned at him.

Holmes said: 'Gare du Nord is littered with campaign posters publicizing a speech Fournier will be giving in Corbie tomorrow lunchtime. We shall go and see him, and find out just how honourable he really is.'

CHAPTER TWENTY-FIVE

The Choice

As Verne's coach took them back through the city towards her hotel, Lydie gave Watson a tremulous smile and said: 'Your friend, M'sieur Holmes ... I do not think he likes me very much.'

Watson put his hand over hers and squeezed fondly. 'It is nothing personal, *mademoiselle.* I am sorry to say that Holmes has a poor opinion of women in general.'

'Why should that be?' she asked. 'And please, *Docteur* ... call me Lydie.'

Watson flushed with pleasure. 'And you may call me John – Jean, if you will.' He paused, trying to think of how to answer her question without demeaning his dearest friend, then said, 'What you must understand about Holmes is this: he is a man wholly governed by logic. And as such, he finds it difficult to understand women, whom he feels are governed more by emotion. He is not a ... the word in English is misogynist, but I don't know how to translate that into French....'

'It is almost the same,' she said. *'Misogyne.'*

'He is not a *misogyne,*' he continued. 'And yet he has an instinctive mistrust of the species. I have only ever seen him show feelings for one woman, an American opera singer ... and even then those feelings were more akin to admiration than to love.'

'How very sad.'

'In some ways, perhaps. And yet I feel he is happier that

way. Any emotional attachment, aside from simple, genuine friendship, would distract him from his work. And his work is everything to him.'

It was exactly the opening she had been waiting for. 'Is that why he is here … Jean? Is he at work on some exciting case at this very moment?'

'We are here for a holiday.'

She eyed him ruefully. '*You* do not trust women either, I see.'

'On the contrary,' Watson said with a chuckle. 'But Holmes's business is his own, and I fear I have already broken enough confidences for one day.'

'Then you are not here to investigate the shooting of M'sieur Verne?' she asked bluntly.

'*What?* Is that what you suspect? *Mademoi–* Lydie, that was merely a coincidence. Holmes and Verne have been correspondents for some time now. We could hardly come to France and not pay him a visit.'

'I thought perhaps….'

'You will make an excellent journalist,' he said approvingly. 'You have an enquiring mind, and a nose for a story. But you will not find one here.' An idea suddenly occurred to him. 'Are you hungry? If you like we could stop off somewhere and have a meal.'

'I should like that very much.'

Watson sat forward and poked his head out the window. 'What is the finest restaurant in all of Amiens, Metier?' he called to the coachman.

Metier considered the question before replying: 'Probably La Mirabelle, *Docteur.*'

'Then take us there at once, if you please.'

'*Oui, m'sieur.*'

The restaurant certainly deserved its reputation. The food was excellent, the service discreet, the surroundings quite charming and the company … well, Watson felt he could have asked for none better. Indeed, he felt a sharp twinge of regret when he finally thought to check his watch and realized that they had lingered far longer than they had planned in their opulent surroundings.

It was a little after seven o'clock when Metier reined up the horses and the coach halted before the grand edifice of the Hotel Cheval Noir. Watson climbed out, took Lydie's hand and helped her down to the pavement. He escorted her into the hotel, Lydie receiving admiring looks from the gentlemen guests, and on through to the reception.

'I hope we shall meet again very soon,' he said.

'It is a hope we share,' she replied. Then impulsively, or so it seemed, she reached up and pecked him on the cheek.

He felt himself flushing. 'Good night, Lydie,' he managed.

'Good night, Jean.'

Watson turned and walked towards the exit. But after only a few steps he looked back, ostensibly to offer one final wave. In fact, he watched carefully, and hated himself for it, in order to obtain her room number.

It was dark when the carriage turned into Rue Charles Dubois and Metier dropped him off at the front gate. Watson stood there, inhaling the cool night air and watching until the coach turned a corner in order to enter the stables by way of a rear entrance. At last he pushed through the gate and started across the courtyard to the house.

'Watson.'

Startled, he turned quickly. For a moment he could not see anyone. Then he caught the familiar strong odour of shag tobacco and saw Holmes standing beneath one of the beech trees to his right, smoking a small-bowled clay pipe.

'Holmes!' he said, coming closer. 'What are you doing out here?'

'Waiting for you, old friend.'

'Me? Why? What has happened?'

'I have discovered – or more accurately confirmed – what is

143

at the heart of this matter. But I am not sure how you will react to it.'

Watson frowned uneasily. 'Then perhaps you had better tell me and we will discover the answer together.'

Still Holmes hesitated, until finally he could hesitate no longer.

When he had finished speaking, Watson stood there, as still and silent as a statue. Then the air left him in a rush and he hissed, so as not to be heard by anyone in the house: 'Good grief! The man's conduct has been both immoral and disgraceful!'

'On the contrary,' said Holmes quietly, 'Verne's only crime has been to submit, perhaps unwisely, to the affection he could not show his own son.'

'His conduct has been abhorrent.'

'The practise of cannibalism among the Melanesian tribes, the ritualized taking of heads by the peoples of China, India, Borneo and others, the custom of shrinking those same dismembered heads as performed by the Jivaro Indians of Ecuador ... these things are also abhorrent to us. But those who do not seek to change the ways of others do the only thing they can – respect their right to practise them.'

'*Condone* such a thing?' Watson shook his head angrily at the very notion. 'Never! And I warn you, I shall find it hard indeed to show Verne any respect after this.'

'Then you are not the man I believed you to be,' Holmes said flatly. 'You, as a doctor, should know better than most all the weaknesses to which man is heir. Do you condemn a patient when he falls ill?'

'Are you trying to tell me that such non-conformism is an illness?'

'I am not. But the medical fraternity considers "non-conformist" behaviour the result of mental disorder and moral deficiency, does it not?'

'So what are you saying? That I should *not* feel outraged by Verne's conduct?'

'As a doctor, you take an oath to treat everyone with the same degree of care and respect, and pass judgement upon no one. Verne is not the first man in history to feel an attraction to both man and woman, and he will not be the last. One day, society may feel less inclined to judge and ostracize such people. But until that day comes, it is a heavy load to bear. The least you and I can do for Verne is make that load somewhat lighter. He is above all else a good man, Watson, a decent and kind man.'

'He is a *pillow*man,' said Watson.

Holmes grimaced at the insult. 'You surprise me, Watson. What is the feeling of love for one man to another, when set against that of murder, attempted murder, corruption on a nationwide scale and ruthless, cold-blooded coercion? What is the greater crime here, Watson? That Verne showed love for another man, or that the Knaves took his nephew and drove him even further into insanity so that he would eventually murder his own uncle?'

'I cannot help the fact that I do not share your enlightened attitude,' Watson said stiffly.

'Then you have to make a choice, old friend. You are with me – with *Verne* – in this business for no other reason than that it is the right course to take, or you may go on to Henri Gillet and play out the rest of this holiday alone.'

'You know I would not do that. I would walk through hell itself if you asked me to.'

'All I am asking is that you see Verne not as some vile and unclean monster, but as a man. A good man. A man who deserves our help.'

'All I can promise,' Watson said wretchedly, 'is that I will try. But after this, it will not be easy.'

'You may change your mind before this is over,' Holmes predicted. 'Now – where is the Denier woman staying?'

'You're wrong about her, you know.'

'I am seldom wrong, especially when the facts speak for themselves. Again I ask – where is she staying?'

'The Cheval Noir.'

'And her room number?'

'Why do you want that?'

Holmes made no reply, just stared at him through a rising haze of tobacco smoke.

At last Watson sighed and said: 'Three-two-four.'

'Thank you. Now come inside. I can see you have already eaten; the moustache is not referred to as a soup-strainer without good cause. But Madame Verne's cook has prepared what promises to be a truly excellent *Aile de raie aux câpres,* and you may need all your strength for the morrow.'

'Why? What's happening then?'

'We are going to Corbie,' said Holmes, starting back towards the house. 'And a meeting with François Fournier.'

CHAPTER TWENTY-SIX

— ୧ ୨ —

A Man of Honour

A picnic atmosphere had already claimed Corbie by the time they arrived late the following morning. So many people had turned out to see and listen to Fournier that many of the streets leading to the centre of the small town had been cordoned off to vehicles.

When Metier could drive the carriage no further, Holmes, Watson and Verne had to alight and make their way towards the town square on foot – no mean accomplishment for Verne, who was still using crutches beyond the confines of his own home.

Corbie lay in the valley of the Somme, and was bisected by the canal of the same name. It had grown up around the Benedictine monastery of Corbie Abbey beginning in the late seventh century, and there was ample evidence of its long history to be seen everywhere.

Men, women and children had all turned out in their Sunday best for the forthcoming speech, many of them having made the journey from neighbouring Villers-Bretonneux. Wary *gendarmes* prowled among them, looking for troublemakers and anarchists, while reporters busily scribbled word-pictures of the scene in their notebooks.

Over everything a carnival spirit seemed to prevail that reminded Watson of their first few hours in Amiens. Many of the locals had decided to hold impromptu street parties, and had set up trestle tables that were weighed down with food. Bunting strung across the streets flapped and waved gaily in the stiff breeze. Someone was even running a tombola. The air smelled of cheese and fruits, of homemade chocolate truffles, croissants, doughnuts, muffins and those succulent coconut biscuits known as *congolais*.

In the town square the local brass band struck up a spirited rendition of *Le Marseillaise*. Holmes and his companions followed the music until they came to a temporary stage draped in the amethyst and amber party colours of the Independent Republicans, behind which two medium-sized marquees had been erected. People were already drifting in from the surrounding sights and amusements in readiness for the moment when François Fournier finally took the stage and made one of the impassioned speeches for which – according to Verne – he was famous.

'I still think we're taking a damnable chance,' muttered Watson, trying to keep a watch on everyone around them. 'I feel like Daniel in the lion's den.'

'And yet I believe we are safer here than we have been throughout this entire affair,' Holmes replied. 'The Knaves will not try anything at the moment. There are too many witnesses. And as powerful as they are, even they cannot browbeat or bribe an entire town.'

'I wish I could be sure of that.'

Since the previous evening his attitude towards Verne had grown noticeably cooler. He was civil to the author and spoke when spoken to, but offered no more than that. Verne, sensing that Holmes had told him everything, had tried to accept Watson's lack of warmth philosophically. But it was obvious that he was deeply hurt by the breakdown of their growing friendship, though he made no comment about it.

Gradually they worked their way to the front of the crowd, then at Holmes's urging they edged to one side of the stage, where the crowd wasn't quite so compressed. Their view here was good. A lectern had been set up in the centre of the stage, this also draped with the colours of Fournier's party.

Suddenly the band fell quiet. All that could be heard now was the muttering of the crowd. A few of them were waving pro-Fournier banners above their heads. More *gendarmes* were working through the assembly, still on the lookout for any de Freycinet supporters who might try to disrupt the proceedings.

Off to their right a curtain twitched and a moment later a tall, elegant-looking man with white hair and a forked beard strode to the lectern. He wore a well-cut pale grey suit, white shirt and a blue cravat. Holmes was immediately attentive, for this man matched the description of the man who had visited Gaston Verne the week before his supposed 'escape' from the sanatorium. The crowd grew quiet save for the odd wail of a baby, or the expectant clearing of a throat.

'My friends!' began the man, and then paused to make sure everyone was attentive.

Holmes studied him, looking for the Knaves' distinctive tie pin but failed to see it. 'I am so pleased to see you all here today, and I rejoice in the good common sense you have shown in coming to hear what M'sieur Fournier has to say about the state of our country and what needs to be done – what François Fournier himself will do – to put things back to rights! And so, may I present the man I believe will be the next prime minister of France – François Fournier!'

The band immediately struck up a rousing military march. Caught up in the excitement, the crowd burst into applause, drowning the few cat-calls from Fournier's opposition. There was a moment when nothing happened; Fournier was clearly delaying his entrance for dramatic effect. Then the curtain stirred again and a young man in his mid-twenties came out and started waving at the crowd. He was tall and spare, with a long face, a well-defined jaw and a beaming politician's smile. His skin was tanned, his eyes the palest blue, his nose straight, his lips full. He wore his thick, blue-black hair with a left-side part.

He went to the lectern and shook hands with the white-haired man, then faced his audience. Once again the band stopped playing and slowly the cheering and applause died down.

'My friends,' he said, voice deep, clear and powerful, 'it is no secret that I feel passionately about this great country of ours. That is why it grieves me to see the sorry state into which we are slowly but surely descending. Of course, you are all familiar with M'sieur de Freycinet. In his first term as *premier ministre français* he lasted for nine months before his profligate ways and reckless expenditure forced him to resign. Upon his second term, his disastrous handling of foreign affairs effectively ended our influence as a worldwide power. And yet the typically generous spirit of the French people has allowed him back for a third time, and in as many months he has broken promise after promise, pledge after pledge, and is now struggling to hold his own party together! I ask you, if a man cannot even do that, how can he hope to hold his *country* together?'

He fell silent until the surge of cheering, whistles and applause died down again.

'We have to change, my friends. And we cannot delay. We have to call a vote of no confidence in Charles de Freycinet and elect a new party to power, one that will put the country before itself. But I understand your scepticism where politics is concerned. Do you know something? I share that scepticism, and I *am* a politician!

'So what do I stand for? What will the Independent Republicans do for you, if we are privileged enough to receive your vote?

'I'll tell you.

'Firstly, we will establish a system of law and government that treats every man, woman and child as an equal. We will curb government interference and allow the businessmen of the country to expand and in so doing create jobs and wealth.

'Do we need an army? Can we *afford* an army? Yes! But it will be a smaller one, and more wisely deployed, for we shall seek always to use diplomacy over force. We want to see a five-day working week, a working day of no more than eight hours, the complete abolition of child labour. We need to educate our young people in all the traditional subjects, but more than that we need to teach them a responsibility to society. We need to take our banks, our railways, our mines back into state owner-ship, make our tax system fairer.

'Now, these are just grand words – at the moment. And unless you call for the resignation of M'sieur de Freycinet and vote for the Independent Republicans, all they will ever be are empty promises. You must choose simply between what you already know to be a failed system of government, and find the courage to install a new one. My friends – thank you!'

Again the crowd erupted, and again the band started playing *Le Marseillaise*. As Fournier waved to his audience, Watson leaned close to Holmes and said: 'Well, you certainly cannot argue with his policies.'

'Not at all,' Holmes replied. 'If he is sincere in his desire to carry them through. But promises are cheap, and it has been the sad experience of one electorate after another that politi-cians will say anything to acquire the votes needed to bring them to power. Then they practise selective amnesia.'

Fournier turned and started to leave the stage. Holmes turned to Verne and said: 'Call to him!'

Earlier they had agreed that this was their best chance to obtain an audience with the man. Had they requested a meeting beforehand, Fournier's staff could have simply fobbed them off, even someone as famous as Verne. But to use the politician's own trick against him – to buttonhole a man when he least expected it – was to give him no chance to refuse.

'*François!*' called Verne. And again: '*François!*'

At first Fournier seemed not to hear the writer. Then Verne called his name a little louder. Fournier glanced around blankly, then down towards the sound of the voice. Recognizing Verne, he promptly stopped. Holmes watched his expression. In it he seemed to read surprise, then alarm, then – and this was the last thing he had been expecting – undisguised pleasure.

To the astonishment of the crowd, Fournier hurried to the edge of the platform and leapt down to the ground. He clasped Verne by the forearms, his smile making him look even more boyish.

'Jules! I read about what happened. My God, man, how are you?'

'I am improving by the day,' Verne said, adding: 'François, please allow me to introduce my friends Sherlock Holmes and Dr Watson.'

Fournier's eyes widened. '*The* Sherlock Holmes?'

'I do not believe there is another,' said Holmes.

'I am delighted to make your acquaintance, sir. Yours too, *Docteur*. But what are you doing here, Jules?'

'We would be grateful if you would give us a few moments,' said Verne.

Fournier grimaced. 'I wish I had those moments to spare, but my campaign manager is keeping me on the move. I have to shake hands and kiss babies in just a moment, and then I am off to Châtillon-sur-Marne to deliver another speech.'

'I am afraid I must insist,' Verne said firmly.

Fournier frowned, puzzled by his old friend's insistence. But before he could reply, the white-haired man came hurrying across the stage and looked down at them in an impatient way that made Watson believe he was used to getting his own way. 'Is there something the matter here, François?' he barked.

Fournier looked up at him. '*Non*. Alexandre, this is my very good friend Jules Verne, and his friends Sherlock Holmes and Dr Watson. Gentlemen, this is my campaign manager, Alexandre Absalon.'

Absalon continued to glare down at them. He paid particular attention to Holmes. 'I am afraid I must remind you of our schedule,' he said to Fournier.

'Of course. Nevertheless, I should like to spare these men a few moments.'

'Alone,' said Holmes.

Fournier frowned at him. 'Of course. Gentlemen, please come this—'

'François,' said Absalon, a hint of censure in his tone. 'This is highly irregular.'

'Perhaps. But I do not believe these gentlemen have been sent by the Opportunist Republicans to convert me to their cause, have you, gentlemen?' He smiled again, adding: 'Please, step this way.'

He led them into one of the marquees that had been erected behind the stage and was now decked out as a crude temporary office. There, he asked his campaign staff to leave them alone. As he pulled the flap down behind them, the sounds of the cheering crowds and their brass band accompaniment were suddenly muted.

'Jules,' Fournier said again, 'what is the meaning of all this?'

It was Holmes who answered. 'We have come to issue an ultimatum, M'sieur Fournier. We know practically everything about the activities of the Knaves and their attempt upon M'sieur Verne's life, and we have taken steps, in the form of a comprehensive dossier upon the activities of the group, to make sure they leave him alone.'

Fournier scowled at him. 'You have me at a disadvantage, *m'sieur.*'

'Then I shall make it as simple as it can be,' Holmes said. 'In the event of M'sieur Verne's death by any other than natural means, as well as those of Dr Watson and myself, certain trusted parties have instructions to make the aforesaid dossier known to the police agencies both in France and across Europe.'

It was, of course, a bluff, but Holmes was hoping that it would serve a dual purpose – to afford Verne a degree of safety, and to force the Knaves into doing something rash that he, Holmes, might then use to his advantage.

But again Fournier surprised him. 'I am sorry, *m'sieur,* but I have no idea what you are talking about. Who or what are the Knaves? What has this dossier got to do with me?'

Holmes stared at him for a long moment. He had the sense that Fournier was being completely honest with them. He remembered what Verne had said about the man. *You are wrong about Fournier. I am sure of it! He was always a man of honour, and he would never do anything to harm his beloved France.*

He said: 'Who is backing your campaign, M'sieur Fournier? Who is *really* behind the Independent Republicans?'

'We are a political party like any other, M'sieur Holmes. We are comprised of men from all walks of life, who object to the reckless and haphazard manner in which the country is presently being governed. As for any issues of fund-raising, you will have to ask Alexandre.'

'Very well, *m'sieur.* Let us lay our cards on the table – beginning with the Knave of Hearts.'

'I do not follow.'

'There is a group at work in this country who seek to obtain the power to rule, through you. They chose you to run for the premiership because you were the most likely candidate to give them the victory they sought. But you were doubtless the subject of certain … enquiries … before your candidacy was confirmed. These men have invested a considerable amount in getting you to the Hotel Matignon,' he said, referring to the prime minister's official residence. 'They would want to ensure that you are beyond reproach.'

'I should like to think that I am,' said Fournier.

'But we all have skeletons in our closets, *m'sieur.* Indiscretions, perhaps. Were you asked about your own?'

Fournier's eyes moved infinitesimally towards Verne, who said gently: 'Did they ever enquire about your relationship with me?'

Fournier paled. 'I am sorry, gentlemen. I do not wish to be rude, but I see no reason why I should discuss—'

Verne said flatly: 'They already know, François. And M'sieur Holmes has reason to believe that these men, these so-called Knaves, were behind the plot to kill me.'

Fournier turned even paler. 'What?' he whispered.

'Was your relationship with M'sieur Verne called into question?' demanded Holmes.

His mind elsewhere, Fournier said vaguely: 'Yes. I explained that Jules and I had enjoyed a close friendship – no more – and they seemed satisfied with that.'

'Nevertheless, they believed, rightly or wrongly, that there was more to it than the friendship of one man with another, and they took measures to remove the only other player in that relationship to protect you – more accurately, *them* – from any future embarrassment.'

'No!'

'I fear that M'sieur Holmes is right, François,' Verne said in defeat. 'He has uncovered evidence that cannot be disputed.'

'And you think that I would be a party to such an outrage?' demanded Fournier. 'I shall summon Alexandre at once, and we will get to the truth of the matter!'

'You will say nothing,' Holmes insisted. 'And for one very simple reason. The agents of this group are everywhere. In all likelihood, your M'sieur Absalon is one of them. He certainly fits the description of the man who visited Gaston Verne the week before he allegedly escaped from the sanatorium where he was being held and made the attempt upon his uncle's life. No; question them now and they will do one of two things – attempt to induct you into their organization, or kill you, taking pains to make your death appear quite natural, should you refuse. For your own safety, I advise that you feign ignorance of their true motives, until we can bring about their downfall.'

'They have used me, then,' said Fournier, his mind still elsewhere. 'Damn them, they have pretended to share my vision of the future and all the time I have been nothing more than a means to an end, a puppet to be manipulated.'

'I am afraid so,' said Verne.

'Well, I appreciate your advice, M'sieur Holmes,' Fournier said, his voice now low and choked with anger, 'and I will take it – to a point. But I cannot just allow this group to grow unchecked. They have used me as they plan to use France herself. I will not stand for that, but fight them with every breath I have.'

'Then again, I urge you to say nothing,' Holmes counselled. 'You may be more valuable to us where you are.' He paused thoughtfully and then said: 'You have attended meetings with these men in the past?'

'I suppose I have, albeit without realizing it.'

'Where?'

'All over France.'

'Any one place in particular? They must have a headquarters somewhere. If we can discover that, the very place from which they operate, then we have a chance of breaking them.'

Fournier said hesitantly: 'There is one place. I didn't think much of it at the time, but it is certainly set away from prying eyes.'

'Where is it?' Holmes asked.

Fournier was just about to tell him when Alexandre Absalon ducked inside, an expensive fob watch in his palm. 'I am sorry, gentlemen, but we really are on a very strict itinerary.'

Holmes looked Fournier in the eye. 'Certainly. Well, thank you again for your time, M'sieur Fournier. I wish you luck in your campaign.'

Fournier squared his shoulders and nodded. 'I am glad of the opportunity to meet you, M'sieur Holmes.' And then, doubtless for the benefit of Absalon: 'Jules knows well how much I have always enjoyed reading of your brilliant exploits. It has been a pleasure to meet the protagonist in person – and, of course, the author.'

'We will speak again when your schedule isn't quite so hectic,' said Verne, shaking hands with him.

Fournier nodded. *'Bon chance,'* he said softly.

CHAPTER TWENTY-SEVEN

Know Your Enemy

As they made their way back to Amiens in Verne's carriage, Watson said: 'So – where does that leave us?'

'I must confess, it never occurred to me that Fournier was anything other than a willing accomplice in this business,' said Holmes. 'But I am glad to be proved wrong, for not only does it justify your faith in him, M'sieur Verne, it also gives us an ally among our enemies.'

'But the object of the exercise,' Watson persisted, 'was to convince these people that we know more about them than we actually do, and to make them leave M'sieur Verne alone. We have accomplished neither.'

'Watson, you are usually such an optimistic fellow. Such pessimism is not becoming.'

'Well,' muttered Watson, 'perhaps I have been too optimistic in the past, always ready to see the good in a person.'

Verne glared at him. 'May I take it that that remark was directed at me, *Docteur?*'

'It was a general observation, nothing more.'

'It did not sound like one,' said Verne.

'Then for that I apologize,' Watson said stiffly.

'We still have one other link to the Knaves that we may exploit,' Holmes said thoughtfully. 'Mademoiselle Denier.'

'That woman has nothing to do with this,' Watson said stubbornly.

'Very well,' said Holmes. 'Take her to dinner again – tonight.

And throughout the evening feed her just enough clues to imply that we are involved in a case right here in Amiens and are closing in upon the guilty party by the moment. Puff the thing up, make it appear that we know more than we actually do, and then gauge her reaction.'

'I do not care to use the lady in that manner.'

'Then do it in order to prove her innocence. If she really is as blameless as you claim, there is no harm in the deception. If, on the other hand, you provoke a reaction from her, well, it is as Sun Tzu tells us – know your enemy.'

'What about M'sieur Verne, here?' demanded Watson. 'I have my responsibilities as his protector – unless you will take over for this evening?'

'I have other plans,' said Holmes. 'But from all I hear of the man, I should say that your son could cover for Watson this evening, sir.'

Watson considered this. 'He *is* the man for the job,' he told Verne. 'He would give his very life for you.'

'Let us hope it doesn't come to that,' said Verne.

'Then it is agreed,' Holmes said.

'I'll do it,' Watson granted through clenched teeth. 'But only so that I may have the satisfaction of proving you wrong, Holmes.'

Upon their return to Amiens, Watson sent a note to Lydie at the Cheval Noir, inviting her to dinner that evening. A part of him hoped she would claim a prior engagement. But her reply came within the hour; she said she would be delighted to accept, and that she would be waiting for him to collect her at 7.30.

He arrived promptly on time, and as the carriage took them towards the centre of town and a restaurant recommended by Verne, he looked at his companion and wondered again how Holmes could possibly suspect her of being in league with the Knaves. If anything, she looked even more enchanting tonight than she had at any other time during their acquaintance.

But Watson reminded himself that he was here for a dual purpose. Spending time with such a spectacularly beautiful woman was no chore, but the act of feeding her information in order to reveal whether or not she was indeed an agent of the Knaves was extremely distasteful to him.

'I am so glad you accepted my invitation,' he confessed.

'I was glad to receive it,' she replied. 'You are fortunate, Jean. You are not here all by yourself. You have Holmes and M'sieur Verne for company. I have no one.'

'It must be lonely for you. But when you return to Paris with your interviews, I rather suspect that M'sieur Constantin will be only too pleased to give you the career you seek.'

'His name is Jarnett,' she corrected automatically. If she suspected that he had deliberately made the same mistake as Holmes in an effort to catch her out, she gave no indication of it. 'I must say, you have been most generous in allowing me to interview you.'

'Verne, certainly,' he replied. 'But not I.'

'Don't underestimate yourself, Jean. You are a writer, and a good one.'

'I think Holmes might disagree with you there.'

'Holmes.... Perhaps I shouldn't say so, but I find him a disagreeable man in every respect.'

'Holmes is ... well, *Holmes,* I'm afraid. But perhaps he is rather more mordant than usual because of the case he is working on.'

'I know better than to ask you for details of the matter,' she said, smiling.

Reluctantly he took the opportunity he had been seeking. 'Secrecy is vital during an investigation,' he explained. 'But now that the investigation has been all but concluded ... well, it can do no harm to give you a vague outline of the matter.'

She raised her perfect eyebrows in surprise. 'I take it as a great compliment that you would trust me so much.'

The words were like a dagger to him, but he pressed on,

hating himself for it. 'We have stumbled across a plot to seize control of the country.'

'*Non!*'

'Oh yes. There is a group of very powerful men at work here, and they are interested in nothing but accumulating wealth and power at the expense of France. Furthermore, they will stop at nothing to achieve it, including cold-blooded murder.'

She considered that for a moment, eyes wide, then said: 'Are you telling me that the attempt upon M'sieur Verne's life was somehow part of that plot?'

'I can neither confirm nor deny. But let us say that we are closing in on them now. Holmes has amassed a wealth of information upon them, and expects to have the entire group apprehended before the week is out.'

'Who are they, these people?'

'They are known as the Knaves,' he said, watching her closely for a reaction. In the darkened coach he saw none.

'This all sounds thrilling,' she allowed at last. 'Is it the activities of these Knaves that brought you to France in the first place?'

'Partly,' Watson lied. 'We have been charting their progress for a number of months now, waiting for the right moment to make our move against them.'

'Be careful, Jean,' she said, reaching out to lay one delicate hand on his.

He felt a tingle of pleasure that his welfare should mean so much to her. 'Enough talk of such a dark subject,' he said. 'Tell me all about yourself, Lydie. I want to know everything about you.'

'There is not that much to tell.'

He squeezed her hand again. 'I am sure you're being too modest. I have the feeling that a man could never stop discovering new things about you, Lydie.'

CHAPTER TWENTY-EIGHT

Confirmation

As soon as the carriage pulled away from the Cheval Noir, a man stepped out of the shadows of a shop doorway on the other side of the road. He quickly crossed over to the hotel and vanished into a darkened alley next to the building.

The alley led to the back of the premises, where a loading bay – empty at this time of night – stood beside a yard cluttered with broken furniture and dustbins. Bars of light slanted through a row of small sash windows to puddle on the flagstones, and because the windows were all open there also came the clanking and clinking of pots and pans, waiters calling orders, the occasional hiss of some delicacy being thrown into a hot *poyle*.

The man waited a moment, then leapt lightly onto the loading bay. His shadow grew large as he approached the double doors at its far end. Then he turned slightly towards what little light there was and produced a small toolkit from the pocket of his black double-breasted frock coat. From this he selected what looked like a scalpel blade, to the end of which was attached a long, thin metal pin, and a thin tension wrench of similar dimensions.

For twenty seconds the man worked the tension wrench to left and right, testing the firmness of the stop in the lock. He worked gently and with great sensitivity until he was fairly certain which direction he had to work towards. Finally he traded the tension wrench for the pick, and went to work locating and then pushing each individual pin up until, with a soft click, it set.

In less than a minute he had opened the door and let himself inside.

The storeroom beyond was piled high with boxes, old Christmas decorations and items of furniture that were still in good condition but surplus to requirements. He made no more noise than a thought as he crossed the room to the door in the facing wall.

He opened the door a crack.

Light from a nearby gas mantle illuminated his thin face. The face of Sherlock Holmes.

He left the storeroom and made directly for a darkened, dingy back staircase at the end of the corridor. Taking the steps two at a time, he climbed silently to the third floor, then let himself through a door into which was set a small window. Now he was in a carpeted hallway with a series of numbered doors set opposite each other in the facing walls. He stopped at a door numbered 324 and once again used his pick to force the lock.

Once in the darkened room beyond, he began a systematic and thorough search of Lydie's belongings, but found nothing to link her to the Knaves. A soft sound of frustration escaped him. Then, doggedly, he resumed his search.

There was a slim evening purse tucked into the elasticised pocket of her tan leather suitcase. Inside were a few personal items and a scrap of paper. He took the scrap of paper across to the window and tilted it towards the gas streetlights below so that he could read it. It said:

16/3/86 09:30
Valentin

He replaced the scrap of paper in the purse and put the purse back exactly as he had found it. He reached up and felt across the top of the wardrobe for anything she might have tried to put out of reach. There was nothing. He dropped to his knees, checked under the bed and again found nothing. There was a pine armoire on the other side of the room. He checked every shelf, with similar lack of success.

It was only as he closed the doors on the armoire that he realized it stood upon a shaped apron of wood with splayed feet. Again he dropped to his knees and felt around beneath the wardrobe.

This time the tips of his fingers came into contact with something tucked right at the very back, close to the wainscoting.

He managed to grasp it and slid it out for a closer examination. It was a box about three inches thick, measuring some fourteen inches by nine. It had brass hinges and a small brass lock.

Holmes worked quickly to open it, taking care to leave no tell-tale marks upon the metal. Within moments he was able to lift the lid to reveal two shaped compartments covered in blue velvet.

It was a gun case, constructed to hold two pistols, one of which was now missing.

Holmes recognized the remaining pistol immediately. It was a Perrin and Delmas pistol of 1859 – partner to the one with which Gaston Verne had tried to murder his uncle on 9 March.

CHAPTER TWENTY-NINE

She's Not What You Think She Is

'I tell you, Holmes, you could not have been more wrong about that woman,' Watson said with no small satisfaction. 'She showed *exactly* the level of interest I would have expected from someone of her intelligence and enquiring mind, but no more – and believe me, Holmes, I watched her like a hawk!'

It was shortly after midnight and Watson had let himself into Verne's house to find Holmes waiting for him in the sitting room, sprawled in a chair with his long legs crossed at the ankles, his fingers steepled across his chest.

Watson was in good humour, for not only had he just spent a very agreeable evening in the company of a most attractive woman, he had also proven Holmes wrong into the bargain. It didn't happen often, and he was determined to enjoy every moment of his triumph.

Furthermore, he felt that he had made a real connection with Lydie, whose interest in him seemed entirely genuine. With the distasteful business of 'testing' her out of the way, he had been free to enjoy the rest of the evening; and enjoy it he had, except for one unexpected moment towards the end. He had glanced across the table at her and just before she turned away from him he could have sworn he saw a tear in her eye.

'Are you all right, my dear?' he asked, immediately concerned.

'Yes. Yes, I'm fine.'

'You're *crying*.'

'*Non,*' she said. 'It is just an allergy.'

'Come now,' he said, and reached across the table to cover one of her hands with one of his. 'I am a doctor, remember. You cannot fool me. Have I said something to offend you?'

'Of course not. You have been the perfect companion. Truly. And that is the problem.'

'I'm sorry. You have lost me.'

Lydie hesitated, not sure how to describe her feelings. 'It's just that … you know something about me now, Jean, how I lost my parents when I was still young, and how I have had to struggle ever since in what is a man's world. I know I am not the only one who faced hardship growing up, so do not think that I feel sorry for myself. But I suppose my world has always been one where men use women and women use men. Everyone finds a use for everyone else. But in you, I sense … something unique. You have no other desire in life than to be … kind … decent.'

'Oh, there are plenty of things I desire,' Watson said, trying to make light of it. 'But that should never stand in the way of good manners and regard for others.'

'There, you see!' she said, and gave a teary kind of chuckle. 'A good man. A decent man. A man of modesty who seeks always to do what is right for no other reason than that it is the right thing to do.'

'I think you make too much of it,' he protested.

'No, Jean. You are unique in my experience. And for that I weep – because had I found a man like you years ago, I think things might have turned out very differently for me.'

He could think of nothing to say to that, so he said the only thing that came to him: 'Better late than never.'

She nodded morosely. 'But what happens when you return to England and I return to Paris?'

'Why should that signal the end of our relationship? We can correspond. It is a relatively short journey from England to here. I can come over at almost any time. And you can also come to visit me.'

'The way you talk,' she said, and there was a curious tone of wonder in her. 'You actually include me in your future.'

'Why should I do otherwise?'

'No reason, I suppose. But enough of such silliness.' With effort she fought off her brown study. 'Tell me some more about your experiences in Afghanistan....'

'Watson,' said Holmes, interrupting his friend's reverie. 'Sit down.'

Watson frowned at him, not liking his companion's tone. He sank slowly onto the sofa and said: 'What is it?'

'While you were dining with Mademoiselle Denier, I searched her room.'

'Holmes! That is a damnable thing to have done.'

'Perhaps. But what I found there confirms beyond all doubt that she is indeed in the employ of the Knaves.'

Watson said nothing for a long, heavy moment. The only sound was the crackle and spit of the dying fire. At last he asked unsteadily: 'And what was that?'

'A pistol – the mate of the one Gaston used in his attempt to kill Verne. And a scrap of paper containing a message from a man named Valentin, which may or may not be of relevance, concerning something that is scheduled for half-past nine tomorrow morning.'

'And that is your proof?'

'Is it not enough?'

'Not for me, no. The note ... it could mean anything. A hair appointment, for example.'

'And the gun?'

'Perhaps it was planted there. To throw you off the scent.'

'You don't believe that any more than I do,' said Holmes, rising.

'Damn it, man, Lydie is not what you think she is!'

Holmes looked down at him. 'I wish that were true. But you must watch yourself around that woman. She is part of a ruthless group, and in all likelihood as ruthless as the worst of them.'

Watson sat glumly staring into the embers.

Holmes went to the door, looked back and said firmly: 'Have a care tomorrow, Watson.'

'Eh? Why? Where will you be?'

'I have to leave town for the day. But I am sure I shall return before tomorrow evening.'

He left before Watson could question him further.

CHAPTER THIRTY

—❦—

Valentin's Day

Watson spent a restless night and woke early the following morning with a head that felt as heavy as his heart. He washed and shaved, then dressed and went downstairs. He had no appetite to speak of, and decided that a brisk walk might blow away some of his cobwebs. Since Michel had agreed to stay over, he felt that Verne was in safe hands.

The new day was chilly and overcast. The park where the carnival had been held a week earlier was now all but deserted. City cleaners were gathering up litter. Watson thought about everything that had happened since they arrived and could hardly credit the way his plans for Holmes's relaxing, recuperative holiday had turned out. Then he thought about Verne and the way he, Watson, had changed towards the man when he had learned the truth about the writer's sexuality. He found it so vile that instinctively he tried *not* to think about it.

And yet he could not deny that he liked Verne. He was, as Holmes had reminded him, decent and honourable, and as a doctor he should no more have blamed him for his condition than he would blame a patient for contracting cholera, consumption, or typhus.

For much of the century, such behaviour as Verne had confessed to had been punishable by death, though it had been a good fifty years or so since the last execution had been carried out.

Indeed, now that he thought about it, it seemed a harsh punishment indeed for a crime that was, essentially, the love of one man for another. He had never really considered the unfairness of it until this moment. His upbringing told him that he should consider such men as degenerates. But could he honestly say that *Verne* was a degenerate? Of course not.

He realized then that he was not as tolerant a man as he had always supposed and resolved to change his ways. He was clearly not the 'decent' man Lydie considered him to be.

Lydie....

With her name came even more troubling thoughts.

Much as he wanted to believe that Holmes was mistaken about her, he knew that he could not deny the evidence. To begin with, she had arrived on the same train as Gaston. Did that mean the Knaves had sent her to watch him and make sure he carried out his mission to kill? He found it painful to even consider such an idea. But she had been in the crowd when he had first tended to Verne. And when Verne had survived the shooting, she had approached them on the pretext of being a journalist, perhaps as a way to get close enough to Verne to finish the job Gaston had started.

No – he couldn't, *wouldn't* see her as a killer. She might work for the Knaves, but not as an assassin. Of that he was sure.

But what of the weapon Holmes had found in her hotel room – a weapon that was the very match of the one Gaston had used in his attempt to murder Verne?

He didn't know *what* to think. Ever the man of action, he considered going directly to her hotel and demanding to know the truth. Was Holmes right? And those things she had said about him, about how *decent* he was. Had they been mere words, another attempt to get close to her intended target?

But he knew better than to put Holmes's investigation at risk. All he could do was wait to see how things developed.

He paid for his coffee and untouched croissant and limped

forlornly back towards Rue Charles Dubois. He felt that he was behaving like a lovesick schoolboy and hated himself for it.

His mood was little better by the time he reached Verne's house and rang the bell. Michel answered the door for him. 'You were the early bird today, *oui?*' the younger man said by way of greeting.

'I had a headache,' Watson replied vaguely. 'I thought a walk might clear it.'

'And did it?'

'Not so's you'd notice. Is everything all right here?'

'*Oui,*' said Michel, following him into the hallway. 'An attendant arrived from the hospital a short time ago to change the dressing on Father's leg, but that is all.'

Watson nodded, his thoughts still elsewhere. It was only by chance that he happened to glance at the grandfather clock in the corner and note the time.

It was twenty-five minutes to ten.

He was suddenly struck by an uncanny sense of foreboding.

Holmes had said something about a note in Lydie's room, a note carrying today's date and the time 9.30.

'Where are they?' he demanded suddenly.

Michel gave him a curious look. 'Pardon?'

'Where are your father and this hospital attendant?'

'Upstairs. Father was working when the attendant arrived and I showed him up there—'

But Watson was no longer listening. He flung open the door to the spiral staircase and took the stairs as fast as his game leg would allow. He burst into Verne's small workroom, found it empty and careened on, almost tearing the library door off its hinges in his haste to reach the man whose life he had undertaken to protect.

Verne was sitting on the leather couch below the sash window. A man of about thirty was hunched over his wounded leg. Verne's left trouser-leg had been pulled up and the bandage removed to reveal an angry-looking wound that had been stitched shut but had yet to close completely. The younger man, presumably the hospital attendant, was just about to inject something into the area.

He straightened up quickly, startled as the door slammed back against the wall. He had dark, pocked skin and hollow cheeks, small, heavy-lidded hazel eyes and short, raven-black hair. He was dressed in a cheap grey suit and there was a small medical bag on the carpet at his side.

Watson snapped: 'Just a moment!'

Verne frowned. *'Docteur?* What is the –?'

Watson approached the attendant, demanding: 'What are you doing?'

The attendant got to his feet, thoroughly cowed by Watson's stern manner. 'I am cleaning M'sieur Verne's wound, sir, as I have been told to.'

'You have examined it?'

'Of course, sir.'

'Have you found any evidence of infection?'

'No, sir.'

'Swelling?'

'No, sir.'

'The stitches are all intact?'

'Yes, sir.'

'What are you using to cleanse the wound?'

The attendant blinked at him. 'I don't—'

'What is in the syringe?' Watson demanded.

'Permanganate of Potash, sir.'

Watson fixed him with a hard glare. 'You're lying!'

The attendant recoiled as if slapped.

'You're lying,' Watson repeated, adding: 'Valentin.'

At the sound of his name – the name used to sign the note Holmes had found in Lydie's hotel room – the 'attendant' realized the game was up. Watson saw a nerve twitch in the man's left cheek, and then Valentin threw the syringe at him as if it were a dagger.

Watson lurched to one side and the syringe flew through the open doorway and on into Verne's office, shattering against the wall. With Watson off-balance, Valentin darted for the door. Watson leapt at him and they fell against a wall filled with shelves. Valentin grabbed him by the shoulders and for frantic seconds they grappled with each other, dislodged books tumbling about them. Then Valentin wrenched Watson around and slammed him against the table in the centre of the room.

Watson grunted with pain and staggered backwards. By the time he had recovered, Valentin was running out the door. Watson charged after him. He caught up with him on the landing, just as he reached the head of the stairs, and spun him around. Valentin tried to butt him but Watson jumped back, avoiding him, and swung a roundhouse punch.

Valentin blocked it, grasped Watson by the lapels and pushed him backwards.

Watson stumbled, steadied himself with the banister and was able to grab hold of Valentin's sleeve as he started down the spiral staircase. He jerked Valentin back. The assassin's sleepy eyes were large now, filled with fury.

He lashed out and Watson's right eye and cheek immediately went numb. He fell back, his eye stinging and watering, lunged forward, again grabbed at Valentin's lapel.

They tussled some more, their feet drumming a frantic tattoo against the floorboards. Then Watson broke the other man's grip and caught him with a hard right jab. Valentin made a sound of pain and stumbled back towards the head of the stairs.

He lost his footing and fell headlong. As he crashed and rolled from step to step, the sound he made was almost deafening in the confines of the round tower. At the foot of the staircase he rolled over and hunched himself into a ball, his chest heaving.

*

173

At just that moment Honorine and Michel came running, the black spaniel barking around their feet. Michel, still thinking Valentin was a hospital attendant, actually helped the man regain his feet.

'Hold him!' yelled Watson as he charged down the staircase.

Michel attempted to grab Valentin, but the assassin spun around and sent him sprawling with a punch. Then, holding his left arm tight to his side, Valentin hurried through the conservatory hall, kicking over potted plants as he went in order to delay his pursuer. He tore open the door and ran for the gate on the far side of the courtyard.

By the time Watson burst outside, Valentin was just vanishing through the gate. He knew he could never catch the man, but he had to try. He limped quickly to the gate, wrenched it open, ran as best as he could to the corner of Boulevard Longueville and stopped. He looked in all directions.

But wherever Valentin had gone, he had disappeared completely.

'Dash it!'

Winded, he limped back to Verne's house. Michel had also raced out in pursuit and now demanded to know what had happened. Watson confided his suspicions.

Michel went white with anger. 'Shall I fetch that policeman, what was his name, Mathes?'

'It would do no good now,' said Watson. 'The bird has well and truly flown.'

In any case, Watson had a more pressing concern at that moment. They went back into the house and climbed the stairs to Verne's library. As they entered, Honorine had just finished helping Verne to slip his left foot back into the boot he had removed prior to his 'treatment'. The author immediately shifted forward on the sofa and said anxiously: '*Docteur!* Are you all right?'

Watson looked at him as if seeing him for the first time.

Though another attempt had just been made on his life, Verne was more concerned for the welfare of his bodyguard than himself. Watson felt a flush of shame for the distance he had deliberately put between them.

'At the moment I am more concerned for *you,* sir,' he answered. 'Did that fellow get a chance to inject you?'

'*Non.*'

'Did he do anything other than remove your dressing?'

'*Non.* He was only here a few minutes before you arrived.'

Watson nodded in relief.

'*Docteur,*' said Honorine. 'What was he about to do?'

'I suspect he was trying to introduce some sort of infection into your husband's wound that would poison his blood.'

Verne paled. 'Good grief! But ... how did you know he was not really intending to irrigate the wound with ... what did he call it?'

'Permanganate of Potash? Simple, *m'sieur.* Permanganate of Potash has about it a distinctive purple colour. What was in that syringe looked more like....'

'Yes?'

Watson went through to Verne's workroom and knelt beside the shattered remains of the syringe and its thick, flavescent yellow contents. 'Do you have a microscope, sir?' he called over one shoulder.

'Of course. Here.' Verne indicated a cupboard.

As Watson returned to the library, Michel took a large walnut box from the cupboard. From the box Michel removed a microscope. Watson helped himself to a spare specimen slide and went back to the workroom. As they watched, he carefully scooped up a sample of the syringe's contents and then placed it under the lens.

He studied it for a few moments, then said: 'You have had another lucky escape, M'sieur Verne. Unless I am very much mistaken, the plan was to inject you with a bacterium known as *Staphylococcus aureus.* I recognize it as such from its distinctive shape, which has often been likened to clusters of golden grapes or berries.' He looked from Michel to Honorine and finally settled on her husband, his expression grim. 'Their primary objective was to induce sepsis, or blood poisoning. But even had that not worked, you would almost certainly have contracted pneumonia, meningitis, infection of the bone marrow or thrombic endocarditis. Your death, sir, would have appeared as an entirely natural result of the infection of your wound.'

'An almost perfect murder,' Verne murmured, still in shock.

'But where did that … that man obtain such a bacterium?' asked Honorine.

Watson's face grew grimmer still. 'We are indeed dealing with clever men and subtle means.' He gestured to the liquid on the slide he had just examined. 'What we have here is an exudate, taken in all likelihood from an abscess.'

'You mean that it is … *pus*?'

'Yes,' Watson confirmed. 'Our "attendant", this man whose name is Valentin, doubtless drained it from a patient at your nearest hospital earlier this very morning.'

CHAPTER THIRTY-ONE

La Fôret Domaniale de Malvoisine

As Holmes expected, Lydie left her hotel early the following morning, hailed a cab and drove away.

He did not follow her immediately, and was wise not to do so, for as he had suspected, a second cab came around a nearby corner a few moments later and went in pursuit of her.

In the mouth of an alley across the road from the hotel, Holmes narrowed his eyes as the second cab went past. He could see nothing of the passenger, but it was only to be expected that an organization such as the Knaves would leave nothing to chance. Just as Lydie had been sent here to ensure that Gaston carried out his mission, just as she had been able to locate and order Sergeant Bessette to finish the job, and then later order Bessette's 'lawyer', Prideaux, to kill him before he cracked and spilled whatever he knew about them, so it followed that she too had been shadowed. Holmes realized that Knave agents must be everywhere, each with orders to watch another and ensure that discretion and secrecy were observed at all times.

As the sounds of hoofs and wheels diminished, Holmes returned to his own waiting cab, climbed inside and tapped his cane against the roof. The driver dutifully clucked the horse into motion and set off in pursuit. He was anxious to collect the ten francs Holmes had promised him for following the other cabs without making it obvious.

Lydie's first destination was the telegraph office on Rue

Gambetta. Here she stayed just long enough to send a telegram. Then she climbed back into her cab, her driver turned his vehicle around in the middle of the still largely deserted street and returned the way he had come.

From around the next corner, the second cab dutifully followed after her.

Again Holmes rapped softly on the roof of his cab; again the driver went after them both at a discreet distance.

This time Lydie made directly for Gare du Nord. She alighted before the station, paid the fare and then, pausing only to lift the hem of her grey dress a little so that it would not brush against the ground, hurried inside.

The second cab pulled in behind the first. A tall, long-limbed man in a black suit that was far too short in the arms and legs paid his driver and strode into the station behind her. He was chunky and yet cadaverous, with a long, heavy-featured face, waxy skin and a black derby set atop his close-cropped black hair.

Holmes paid off his own cabbie and waited for a time outside the station. Only when he heard the tell-tale blast of whistles and the slamming of carriage doors did he slip inside. He quickly bought a third-class ticket to Paris – it was the final destination of the only train in the station at this still-early hour – and hopped aboard even as it began to draw slowly away from the platform.

The rail-yards fell behind them and the train picked up speed. At length they crossed the valley of the Oise by way of a bridge with three arches. A long, deep cutting took them on through the stone quarries of St Maximin, and thence across a magnificent viaduct and past a ruined abbey.

But Holmes hardly noticed the scenery. His job today was twofold – to follow Lydie and discover where she was going, and at the same time avoid detection by his target or the man who was following her.

Two hours later the train arrived in Paris. Holmes deliberately hesitated a while before leaving his compartment. When at last he did, he saw with satisfaction that Lydie was just passing through the gates at the far end of the platform, her tall, pale-faced follower not far behind.

Holmes had been right in his assumption that Lydie would travel first-class, and that the man following her would travel by second. Travelling by third-class had ensured that he would not possibly meet up with either of them, even by chance.

The station was all hustle and bustle, but still he was careful to keep his distance and as much as possible remain invisible to those he was following. Outside the station Lydie hurried to an awaiting coach that was black with red wheel-spokes. The driver did not even acknowledge her, but sat on his high seat with his head facing forward. As soon as she got in and closed the coach door, he shook his reins and his two-horse team pulled out into one of the capital's busy thoroughfares.

This time, however, her hulking, cadaverous shadow made no move to follow her. He had doubtless known her destination all along, but had followed her to make sure he was correct. Now apparently he was convinced. Holmes watched him look around, then cross the tree-lined boulevard and enter a post and telegram office. He would now report to his master, doubt-less the man Absalon ... wherever he might be.

Only when he was sure he would not possibly be spotted by the cadaverous man did Holmes finally make his own move. Much to the protests of the drivers lined up ahead of him, he chose the very last cab in the rank and gave the cabbie instruc-tions to follow the black coach. Eager to please, the driver got them moving almost before Holmes was settled in his seat.

They followed the coach through picturesque streets and across bridges, always heading east. About half an hour later they were in the suburbs and the traffic had thinned consid-erably. Ten minutes after that he rapped on the cab roof and the vehicle slowed to a halt, allowing the coach ahead to vanish into thick woodland.

The driver's pinched face appeared in the trapdoor above him. 'What lies beyond those trees?' asked Holmes.

The driver thought for a moment. 'That is la Forêt Domaniale de Malvoisine,' he replied.

'Yes, but what lies *beyond* it?'

The driver shrugged. 'Malperthius ... Saint-Augustin.'

Holmes stared thoughtfully at the clustered oaks. A line of telegraph poles followed the contours of the lane in which they found themselves, until they too vanished into the forest, just as the black carriage had. He remembered something then that François Fournier had said to them the day before. *There is one place. I didn't think much of it at the time, but it is certainly set away from prying eyes.*

'Do you want me to keep following the coach?' asked the driver.

But the chances of being spotted were now too great for that. 'No,' Holmes replied. 'But tell me....'

'*Oui, m'sieur?*'

'Are there any properties located *within* the forest?'

The cab driver gave the question a moment's thought. 'I am not sure,' he answered at length. 'There could be. It covers a large area, you know.'

'Then you may take me back to Paris,' said Holmes. 'I believe my work here is complete.'

CHAPTER THIRTY-TWO

---e⁀⁀⁀---

Forewarned is Forearmed

Seated at the large desk in his ground-floor office, Alexandre Absalon listened in silence until Lydie had finished making her report. Even then he made no immediate response. The prolonged silence grew uncomfortable until at length he finally broke it.

'If this man Watson is to be believed, then Sherlock Holmes is every bit as clever as his reputation suggests.'

She frowned. 'What do you mean – *if* he is to be believed?'

'Do you not think he is using you?' he asked, raising one Mephistophelian eyebrow.

'Certainly not.'

'Then you have been blinded by his charm, Lydie. He is quite the ladies' man, you know. By his own admission his experience of women extends over many nations and three separate continents.'

He watched her closely as he said this, and did not care for the flicker of hurt he saw in her eyes. 'Did you think he was any different to any of the other men you have known?' he asked, his tone deceptively gentle and slightly mocking. 'Did you think he was the *one?*'

'I know that he is a gentleman,' she replied hotly, 'and one who would not find it easy to use another human being.'

'You surprise me. I did not think a woman of your experience could be quite so ... naive.'

'It is not a case of naiveté, M'sieur Absalon. I prefer to think of myself as a good judge of character.'

Although she didn't mean to, she made the statement sound more like an attack on her employer. She thought for a moment that he would censure her, but he didn't. She would have preferred it if he had.

Rising, Absalon walked to one of the windows and gazed out across the magnificent grounds surrounding the chateau. 'This man Holmes knows something,' he said. 'This I know from my own personal experience. But he does not know as much as Watson claims. He cannot. He is bluffing, Lydie. And whether or not Watson was aware of it, he has used his companion to feed you just enough information to make you panic and report directly to me.'

He moved suddenly, quick and fluid as a panther. He crossed to her, grabbed her by her arms, dug his fingers deep into her flesh and shook her as if she were a rag doll. She had never seen him angry. But now he was beyond anger; he was absolutely incensed.

'Were you followed?' he demanded through clenched teeth.

'N-no.'

'Are you *sure*?'

'Of course I am! Stop it! You're hurting me, and I will not stand for that!'

He pushed her away from him. 'You will stand for anything I tell you to stand for,' he rasped. Then: 'But for my foresight, you might well have led them straight to us! That was Holmes's plan! Can't you *see* that?'

She rubbed her arms, knowing that they would be bruised before she returned to Amiens. 'Watson told me enough to convince me that Sherlock Holmes is on to you! I saw it as my duty to report as much at the earliest possible opportunity! Was that wrong of me? Should I have simply remained silent? Forewarned is forearmed, is it not?'

Absalon inhaled angrily. His shoulders rose and fell. He

said: 'You were not followed. I know this, because I have a very special man in Amiens by the name of Sébastien Thayer whose job it has been to follow *you* throughout this entire mission!'

'What?'

He shook his head pityingly at her. 'My God, you really are naive. In this organization, everyone watches everyone else, Lydie. It is the only way to maintain secrecy – and loyalty.'

She wanted to tell him that *he* was naive, too, if he felt that loyalty could be anything other than earned, but she sensed that she was already in enough trouble as it was.

His next statement confirmed it.

'I am all for you using your undoubted charms to carry out the work of the Knaves. That was the purpose for which you were originally recruited. But your feelings for Watson, whatever they may be, have clouded your judgement, and might well have brought about a serious breach of the security we hold so dear.' He paused briefly, then said: 'You have arranged to have Verne's wound contaminated?'

She looked at the spelter clock on the mantelpiece. 'It will have been done by now.'

'Who did you choose for the task?'

'Valentin Faure.'

He nodded, satisfied. Then turning away from her, he said: 'Return to Amiens, collect your things and go back to your *appartement* in Lyon. Do not make any attempt to see Watson again.'

'Why not?'

He waved off her question. 'You are no longer associated with this matter, Lydie. Now, go back to Lyon and wait. The Knaves will find work for you elsewhere, in due course.'

'But I—'

'*Do it,*' he whispered. 'And be grateful that I have shown such leniency.'

She glared defiantly at him for a moment longer. Then deciding not to enrage him further, she silently withdrew.

CHAPTER THIRTY-THREE

An Open Invitation

It was late afternoon by the time Holmes returned to Verne's house. Even before he confronted Watson in the sitting room and saw the bruising around his companion's right eye, he sensed that something had happened in his absence.

'Another attempt was made upon Verne's life,' Watson confirmed upon questioning. He went on to recount the events of the morning, then said quietly: 'I owe you an apology, Holmes. It appears that you, uh ... were right about Lydie.'

'I take no pleasure in that,' Holmes replied bleakly. 'However, she did exactly as I expected her to – she travelled to Paris, and then on to a location either in or beyond la Fôret Domaniale de Malvoisine. Unfortunately I could not follow her to her exact destination for fear of being discovered.'

'But she very nearly led you to the headquarters of the Knaves?'

'That is what I believe.'

Watson cursed under his breath. What a fool he'd been to accept her at face value! And how ridiculous to have clung to the belief that Holmes had been wrong about her in the face of almost overwhelming evidence! He felt immature and thoroughly humiliated. But more than that, he felt disappointed. He had fallen for her glib tongue ... and fallen for her in other ways, too.

'It has been a long day, Holmes,' he sighed, heading for the door. 'I think I will go for a walk.'

'To the Cheval Noir?'

It was on the tip of Watson's tongue to say no, but there was little point: Holmes had always been able to read him like a book. 'If we are to make any real headway in this case, then I think perhaps a little straight-talking with Mademoiselle Denier is in order,' he said.

'She's gone, old friend.'

Watson blinked. 'I'm sorry?'

'Since there was nothing else I could do in Paris, I came back to Amiens ahead of her and awaited her return in a coffee shop across the street from Gare du Nord. When she finally arrived she took a cab directly to her hotel. A little later she reappeared with her bags packed, and returned to the station. There she bought a passage to Lyon.' Again he said: 'She's gone, old friend.'

Watson's brows pinched together. 'Without a word...? But why?'

'Perhaps her presence is no longer needed in this affair. Perhaps word of the second failed attempt upon Verne reached her superiors and she was dismissed.'

Watson's lips thinned. 'I have been such a damned idiot.'

'You are not the first man to allow his heart to rule his head.'

'Not just about Lydie,' Watson replied, lowering his voice. 'About Verne, too ... You know, I was so ready to condemn him, and I *did* condemn him. I still cannot condone his behaviour, of course. I never will. But given the difficult relationship he had with his son, I suppose I can at least ... *understand* it, after a fashion. That was something else you were right about – that I would change my opinion of him.'

'Then you are in credit,' Holmes said gently, 'for you have now learned two valuable lessons from this business, and they can only make you a stronger and wiser man.'

Watson nodded morosely. Holmes may well have been right in what he said ... but just then it was a very small consolation.

That night, over dinner, they discussed Jules and Honorine's forthcoming party at Versailles.

Though Verne himself appeared to have no real enthusiasm for the affair, he was adamant that it should go ahead. Too many people had been invited, he said, and he would not disappoint them. Besides, Honorine had spent weeks planning it. 'There is only one thing I will not do on the night,' he finished, and gesturing to his wounded leg said: 'I very much regret that I will not be able to *dance* with you, my dear.'

'You may surprise us yet,' Honorine said.

The couple had certainly chosen a memorable location for their celebration. The Château de Versailles lay approximately twenty kilometres south-west of Paris. Built by Louis XIV in 1624, originally as a hunting lodge, it had become the home of the French royal family some forty years later and remained so until the Revolution in October 1789.

In the century or so of its royal ownership, four major building campaigns had been undertaken to enlarge and expand the palace until it became one of the largest in the world, and with its 1800 acres of parkland, certainly the largest in Europe.

As Holmes pored over maps of the palace after dinner, the true scale of Versailles became almost too much for even his keen intellect to grasp. The statistics alone were awe-inspiring. Versailles contained more than 700 rooms and very nearly seventy separate staircases. It occupied more than 19,000 acres in total, making it larger than Manhattan Island. Spacious enough to accommodate up to 5,000 people, and with stable-space for 2,000 horses, it also included a faithful replica of a farm, known as Le Hameau de la Reine, to which Marie Antoinette often fled in order to escape the demands of royal life.

It was at Le Hameau that Verne's party was to be held.

'It is a virtual settlement in itself,' he explained. 'There are meadows and streams, a lake, and a number of buildings – a farmhouse, a dairy, barns, a mill, even a tower built to resemble a lighthouse. It is a most unusual location.'

'And your guests will have complete run of this, uh, "settlement"?' asked Watson.

'Of course. The location is too unique to ignore. Weather permitting, I fully expect that most of the festivities will take place out of doors.'

'Where you will be at most risk,' said Holmes.

'And where I will be surrounded by more than seventy family members and friends,' Verne countered. 'Witnesses all, should the Knaves make another attempt upon me.'

'The area should be secure enough,' said Honorine. 'No one will be allowed in without an invitation. Anyone not on our guest list will simply be turned away.'

'That may be true enough,' said Holmes. 'But there will also be caterers, serving staff, musicians – and these we cannot vouch for.'

'Then we will just have to risk it,' Verne said firmly. 'There is no cancelling the event now.'

Holmes studied the map for a moment longer before saying: 'Your staff here can, of course, be trusted?'

'Implicitly.'

'Then we will enlist their help on the day, and place them at strategic points around Le Hameau, with orders to watch for anything suspicious.'

'I too will play my part,' Michel said earnestly.

'We *all* will,' added Watson, smiling at Verne. 'Even, I suspect, Inspector Mathes.'

Without warning, Verne turned away and hobbled to the fireplace.

'Are you all right, Jules?' asked his wife.

He nodded without turning around. 'Yes,' he replied at last. 'But I am humbled. The events of the past week ... Gaston ...

the unwanted attention of these so-called Knaves … well, it has been a trial. And yet here, tonight, I stand among so many good friends, friends willing to lay down their own lives to protect mine.' He turned back to face them, his eyes moist. 'I am indeed blessed,' he said softly.

Later that evening Holmes collected his hat, coat and cane and allowed Watson to accompany him to the door. There, Watson said softly: 'Regardless of what we've said to the contrary, this party of Verne's is an open invitation to the Knaves, you know.'

'Of course it is. But you heard the man. He will not cancel. All we can do is take every precaution as we can to protect him.'

'Just you and I? Verne's son, Inspector Mathes and a handful of domestic staff?' Watson's expression was doubtful. 'Somehow I do not fancy our chances.'

'What choice do we have?' asked Holmes.

Watson made no response. But as he closed the front door behind his friend he thought: *What choice, indeed?*

CHAPTER THIRTY-FOUR

The Loss of a Friend

When Holmes returned to Verne's house the following morning, he received a surprise. As Honorine showed him into the sitting room and then sat beside her husband and Michel on the sofa, she said: 'Docteur Watson left early this morning, *m'sieur*. He said he would not be back until this evening.'

Holmes stared at her. 'Did he say where he was going?'

'No, *m'sieur*.'

'And you did not ask?'

'Surely, the doctor's business is his own.'

'Did he take your carriage?'

'No, *m'sieur*, he left on foot.'

Verne said: 'Is he not entitled to a little time to himself, *m'sieur*? After all, the past week has been a strain for all of us.'

'Watson would not have left your side without good reason.'

'And you are wondering what that reason is?'

'I am indeed.' Holmes knew that for Watson to desert his post at any time, much less now, was wholly out of character and did not bode well. 'Did he receive any visitors either last night or this morning?' he asked.

'*Non.*'

'A note, perhaps?'

'Nothing.'

'And his manner when he left this morning?'

'He was his usual self,' said Honorine. 'Perhaps a little more serious than usual, but....'

189

'He did not appear agitated, as if he were acting upon some sudden impulse?'

'No, *m'sieur.*'

'What can we do?' Michel asked.

Holmes looked at each of them in turn. His face was a mask that betrayed nothing of the very real concern he felt. 'Nothing,' he said calmly. 'I shall attempt to locate him myself.'

Excusing himself, he left the house.

He started at the most obvious point, the Cheval Noir. But the desk clerk was adamant that no one fitting Watson's description had enquired after Mademoiselle Denier either the previous evening or this morning. He asked among the cabbies outside Gare du Nord if they had picked up a passenger of Watson's description that morning. Once again the answer was no. At Gare du Nord itself Holmes asked if a man answering Watson's description had bought a ticket, and if so, where to. The railway clerk told him that he had only come on duty at ten o'clock and really couldn't say.

It was always possible, of course, that Watson hadn't left the city at all. But his comment about returning by this evening implied that he was going further afield. Where? Lyon? It was doubtful. The round trip alone would take at least twelve hours; too far to allow him to return by evening.

Had he remembered something significant that Lydie had told him at dinner the evening before last? Something he had decided to check out by himself? Holmes focused all his energy on solving the mystery, but when he returned to Verne's house two hours later, it was in defeat.

There had been no word from Watson, not that he had really expected any. All they could do was await his return ... and hope that indeed he *would* return.

Watson rang the doorbell a little after seven o'clock that evening. Holmes sprang from his sitting-room chair to answer it. Watson came inside without a word of explanation and took off his overcoat.

'We have been concerned for you,' Holmes said, when it became clear that Watson wasn't about to volunteer any information as to how he had spent his day.

'There was no need. I left word that I would be back this evening.'

'Still, it is out of character for you to simply disappear.'

'I should hardly call it "disappearing",' said Watson. 'It has been a difficult time for everyone. I felt that I needed some time alone, that's all.'

Holmes didn't believe him. There was more to it than that, he felt certain. But he knew better than to pursue the subject. He knew from experience that Watson would under no circumstances appreciate that.

There was to be one more major upset for Verne that week.

The following evening, a Thursday, dinner was interrupted by the sudden appearance of one of Verne's servants. He handed Verne an envelope which he said had just been delivered. Conversation around the table faded as Verne opened the envelope and read its contents. A moment later his shoulders slumped and a curious moan escaped him.

Honorine quickly moved beside him. 'What is it, Jules?'

'It is Hetzel,' he managed at last. 'He is dead.' He bowed his head and murmured: 'Good Lord, will the bad news never stop?'

Later, in the smoking room, the author recovered enough to explain that Pierre-Jules Hetzel had been his publisher for almost a quarter of a century. 'But he was much more than that,' he went on. 'He was a wonderful friend, an astute businessman and the best possible editor any man could wish for. He took a dismal writer and showed him how to really construct his work. He told me to add humour, and I did. He told me to excise great, selfish passages in which I had extolled my own political beliefs, and I did. He dismissed my sad endings and told me to write happy ones, and I did. And through his guidance I became the writer you see before you today.' He swallowed a lump. 'I shall miss him.'

'His death was in no way suspicious?' asked Holmes.

Verne shook his head. 'The man was seventy-two, M'sieur Holmes. He had been in poor health, and the news was not entirely unexpected. But even so, it is hard when a man loses such a friend.'

'We shall cancel the party,' Honorine decided, 'as a mark of respect.'

'No,' said Verne. 'Pierre would never have stood for that. No – the party will go ahead, but in addition to celebrating the thirtieth anniversary of our first meeting, we shall use the occasion to celebrate his memory.'

CHAPTER THIRTY-FIVE

The Queen's Hamlet

It was one thing to study a plan of Le Hameau, but another thing entirely to see the so-called 'Queen's Hamlet' in person.

Tucked away in a remote corner of the palace grounds and further hidden from view by screening belts of trees, it truly was, as Verne had said, a settlement unto itself. As their carriage began its final approach to the location two days later, Holmes and Watson leaned forward in their seats to get a closer look at it.

The terrain had been deliberately landscaped to resemble an idyllic country scene. There was lush meadowland, an orchard and vegetable gardens, rippling streams – even a lake at the centre of which stood a classical Temple of Love.

An octagonal belvedere tower cast its shadow over the rustic scene, and though now in some state of disrepair, the influence of the Norman and Flemish vernacular style of architecture was still plain to see in the buildings situated around the picturesque village pond.

'Good grief,' muttered Watson. 'This is incredible.'

Indeed it was. Here stood a stone farmhouse with a steeply pitched roof, there a dairy. There was a cleared area where a barn had once stood, a dovecote, even a mill that turned lazily within a tower that had been built to resemble a lighthouse.

The late Saturday afternoon was sweet with the scents of shrubs, flowers and lavender, for each of the twelve cottages situated around the pond came complete with either a garden

193

or an orchard. The farm itself had been situated some distance from the hamlet, so that it could be worked as a going concern.

Even now the place was a hive of activity, as workmen clustered in the field before the lake, preparing a firework display that would commence just after sunset. Closer to hand, yet more hired men were planting tall poles at strategic intervals around the hamlet itself, from which lighted torches would supply illumination after dark.

'This,' Verne said, as the carriage came to a halt before the largest house, 'was Marie Antoinette's personal quarters.'

They climbed out and stretched their legs following the long journey from Amiens. Before them stood a two-storey house, into which Verne, now walking reasonably well and using only a cane, led them.

They entered a large room whose panelled walls were hung with fine tapestries. Mahogany furniture from a bygone age was scattered everywhere. A tour of the premises also revealed a backgammon room, a billiard room and a dining room.

Caterers had already started setting up and decorating long, linen-covered trestle tables. Watson ran his eyes appreciatively across the food on offer – everything from plates of Parma ham and Roquefort cheese to roast figs, focaccia buns, smoked salmon, quail's eggs and asparagus salad. In the billiard room a string quartet were tuning instruments and organizing their sheet music.

'What do you think?' asked Michel.

Inspector Mathes, who had travelled with them, shook his head. 'There are too many people around here for my liking,' he grumbled. 'We have to assume they are what they appear to be ... but what if they are *not*?'

Shortly after six o'clock the first of Verne's guests began arriving in their own carriages. The Vernes greeted everyone warmly and showed no trace of the tension they were feeling. Gradually the house began to fill with mingling guests, and the quartet started playing chamber music by Sammartini.

But not every guest arrived by conventional means. As the sky began to darken and the torches were lit, there came a sudden, brief roar of sound to the south and Holmes spun around, startled.

A hot-air balloon was slowly descending from the heavens. Standing not far from Holmes, Watson chuckled as he watched the balloon prepare to land in a field by the lake. 'Unless I am very much mistaken, that will be—'

'Felix Nadar,' said Verne. He shook his head in admiration. 'That man has never obeyed convention in his life.'

Drawn by a subsequent series of similar roars, the other guests wandered outside to watch the balloon drift gently to earth. A few of the men hurried to help Nadar with his anchor and admire the craft at closer quarters. At last the jolly little photographer joined his hosts, kissing Honorine gently on both cheeks and shaking hands firmly with Verne.

'I was so sorry to hear about Pierre,' Nadar said sincerely.

'Yes, he was a good man. Already I miss him dreadfully.'

Almost immediately Nadar brightened. 'And you, *m'sieur,* must be Sherlock Holmes!' he exclaimed. Before Holmes could reply, Nadar grasped his jaw and turned his head sideways. 'I recognized you immediately from Paget's fine drawings! You have a wonderful profile, sir, intelligence of the highest order in every line!'

He turned Holmes's head back so that he could study him face to face, seemingly unaware of the effect his behaviour had upon his subject.

'Please, Felix,' said Honorine, her tone one of long suffering. 'Show some *decorum.'*

But he only waved her away. 'M'sieur Holmes doesn't mind, do you, *m'sieur?* Look, Jules – have you ever seen a more perfect example of scaphocephaly in a human being?'

Realizing that Nadar was essentially drawing attention to the fact that Holmes's head was longer than its width would suggest, Watson could only clear his throat noisily, mutter an excuse about checking the perimeter and turn away before his amusement got the better of him.

He limped along the line of cottages that had been reserved for guests of the queen in days gone by until he reached the last one. Since the Revolution everything had been allowed to fall into ruin, but the place still held a unique atmosphere. He found himself wishing Lydie could have been here to share the experience, and again cursed himself for being a romantic fool.

He remembered Honorine saying to Lydie: 'If you are still here on the twentieth, why don't you come to the ball we're having at Versailles?'

And his own impulsive: 'And I should be delighted if you will allow me to escort you.'

Yes, a romantic fool indeed.

He heard a soft sound behind him and turned just as Holmes strode up, shaking his head and muttering: 'The man is insufferable.'

Watson frowned. 'Verne?'

'*Nadar!* Do you know, he has just likened my "fine brow" to that of *Australopithecus afarensis*!'

'I'm sure he meant it as a compliment,' said Watson, unable to hide his smile.

'My dear fellow,' Holmes replied, 'it is in no way complimentary to be compared to a now-extinct hominid who lived four million years ago! Bah!' He dismissed the very idea with an irritable gesture, adding: 'Well … at least everything here is quiet so far.'

Just then a voice rang out. 'Come on, everyone! Let's go and watch the fireworks!'

They turned in the direction of the voice and saw the party guests begin to leave the hamlet and drift excitedly towards the field in front of the lake.

Holmes scowled. 'I'd feel easier if Verne were not so exposed.'

'At least Michel and Inspector Mathes are keeping an eye on him,' Watson said.

But that was scant comfort to Holmes. 'Come on,' he said purposefully, 'Let's see if we can't between us form some sort of protective shield around him.'

Before they could set off, however, a voice behind them said: 'Champagne, *messieurs?*'

The servant had come upon them almost noiselessly, and as they turned to face him Watson immediately recognized him – his dark, pocked skin and hollow cheeks, his small, heavy-lidded hazel eyes and short, raven-black hair. This was no servant – this was the man called Valentin, who had tried to murder Verne by infecting his leg wound four days earlier.

He was pointing a peculiarly shaped handgun in their direction.

Holmes recognized the weapon immediately – it was a so-called 'apache pistol'; essentially a small 7mm revolver with a knuckle-duster for a handle and a thin knife-blade projecting from just beneath the almost non-existent barrel.

'Don't move,' Valentin hissed. His face still bore the marks of his earlier fight with Watson, and he still held his injured left arm close to his body. 'Do as I tell you and you'll get to live a little while longer.'

'There's nothing you can do to harm Verne here,' Watson told him. 'There are too many witnesses for another one of your "accidents".'

To Watson's surprise, Valentin said: 'It's not Verne we're interested in. Now – turn around, the pair of you, and head for those trees.'

A flick of the revolver's barrel indicated a line of oaks about forty yards east.

Watson tensed. Valentin was no more than a few feet from him. If he could reach him before he could use his gun—

But Valentin somehow divined his intention. For even as Watson prepared to spring, Valentin moved faster. He swung his gun and Watson felt pain explode in his forehead. He staggered back and would have fallen had Holmes not been there to catch him.

'That's for what you did to me last Tuesday,' snarled Valentin.

Watson gingerly felt his forehead. The tips of his fingers came away bloody. 'You swine,' he muttered.

Valentin smiled mockingly. 'Sticks and stones, *Docteur*.' Then, keeping them covered with his gun, he added: 'Move!'

CHAPTER THIRTY-SIX

We're the Targets Now

In a tone that was designed to placate their captor, Holmes said grimly: 'All right. We shan't give you any trouble.' Taking Watson's arm, he helped him towards the woods.

Valentin fell into step behind them.

'Forgive me if I am wrong,' Holmes said over his shoulder, 'but I was under the impression that *Verne* was your target.'

'Things change, *m'sieur.*'

'What things?'

'You'll find out.'

Beyond the flickering torches, the March night was dark. Behind them fireworks began to whiz, whistle and pop hollowly in the sky. The trees drew closer. Trying not to make it too obvious, Holmes slowed his pace in the hope that Valentin would unwittingly close the distance between them. Then he might be able to use his knowledge of *baritsu* to turn the tables on their captor.

But Valentin was an old hand at this game and refused to fall for it. He kept just enough distance between them to make any move Holmes might try suicidal at best.

'Where are you taking us?' Holmes asked.

Valentin's reply was a curious gurgling sound. Before it could properly register with his prisoners, he coughed up blood and fell to his knees. As Holmes and Watson whirled around in surprise, the assassin collapsed on his face at their feet.

The flash of another firework showed them the hilt of a

knife projecting from Valentin's blood-stained back. A second brilliant firework burst above them. By its light they saw the man's killer.

It was Lydie.

Watson felt the blood drain from his face. 'What the deuce—?'

'Shhh,' she whispered. 'I don't think Valentin was alone.'

Kneeling beside the body, she gingerly took the gun from Valentin's nerveless fingers. When she looked up at the men she'd just rescued, she looked pale and shaky. Clearly the act of killing, as opposed to ordering it done, was a new experience for her and one she found repellent.

'Forget about Verne,' she warned them. '*We're* their targets now.'

'I don't understand ...' began Watson.

'I think *I* do,' said Holmes. 'You have changed sides, *mademoiselle*.'

She grimaced. 'I am not that noble, M'sieur Holmes. I was dismissed from my duties. And despite instructions that I return to Lyon and await further orders, I knew that Alexandre Absalon had an altogether different fate in store for me.'

'Absalon!' hissed Watson, remembering the white-haired man they had seen during their audience with François Fournier. 'Then he *is* in league with the Knaves!'

'Did you ever doubt it?' said Holmes. And then, to Lydie: 'You feared for your life.'

'That is the way the Knaves work,' she said simply. 'For as long as you are useful to them, you are safe. But if you fail them, you become a liability. And the one thing Alexandre Absalon hates above all others is a liability.'

'So you fled from Lyon?'

'*Oui.* Absalon had a man following me, a man named Sébastien Thayer. He told me as much at our last meeting. I spotted him when I left Amiens and managed to lose him before we reached Lyon. Then I went to work.'

'Work?'

'I was originally employed for my ability to watch and listen and pick up information,' she said. 'I have built up a vast network of sources, *messieurs,* far more than even Alexandre Absalon suspects. I can help you to bring about the destruction of this group ... if you will trust me.'

Holmes glanced at the dead man. 'One can hardly deny your sincerity,' he said drily.

'So you're only switching sides to save your own skin?' said Watson.

'No, that isn't the only reason.'

'What else then?'

'Before I answer that,' Lydie said softly, 'tell me something, Jean ... was Absalon right when he told me that you were just using me? Feeding me information so that I would lead you to him?'

'Whatever Watson did was at my request,' Holmes inter-rupted. 'And I can assure you that he found the act abhorrent.'

'I did indeed,' Watson said. 'I trusted you and defended you against Holmes's suspicions until I could ignore the evidence no longer.'

Lydie smiled, pleased. 'I am glad to hear it,' she said sincerely. 'I am far from perfect, but I am what my circum-stances and my experience of others have made me. But in you I found someone so different, so reluctant to use or manipulate others for your own ends. It showed me a different and better way to be.'

Holmes said: 'What have you learned, *mademoiselle?* And how may we use it to our advantage?'

'You have heard the news, of course?' she said.

'What news?'

She opened her mouth to speak, but at that same moment the snap of a nearby branch made them turn towards the sound. Lydie instinctively brought up the gun she had just taken from Valentin.

Another firework exploded high above them. The darkness lit up with a shower of falling pink and lavender stars. They caught a glimpse of a figure emerging from the shadows a short distance away – a tall, cadaverous man wearing a black suit that seemed too small for his overlarge body. Instantly, Lydie raised her gun and fired at him.

In her haste she missed.

The man, Sébastien Thayer, did not.

Lydie gasped as the bullet struck her in the chest. She staggered back, dropping her gun, and collapsed.

Overhead a third firework exploded, lighting up the night.

'*Don't move!*' Thayer told Holmes and Watson.

Stunned by the knowledge that Lydie had been wounded, perhaps fatally, Watson ignored him. Quickly kneeling beside her, he gently cradled her in his arms.

'Lydie …' he begged. 'Lydie, talk to me....'

'J … Jean,' she managed.

The light from the firework had faded. But even in the darkness Watson could see that her face was as pale as paper, her only colour coming from the blood flecking her lips.

'S-safe …' she whispered, then winced.

Watson frowned, not understanding.

'Th-the safe,' she repeated thickly. 'It's....'

She died then, with a suddenness that Watson, even with his military experience, had never seen before. No sooner had the last word left her lips than she became absolutely still and her eyes lost all focus and went blank.

For a moment he was absolutely bewildered. 'Lydie ...?' he said urgently, his voice that of a lost child.

Lydie stared emptily into eternity.

Holmes gripped his friend's shoulder. 'She's gone, Watson,' he said. 'And we have no time to mourn her just now.'

'I'm not leaving her,' Watson said.

'Then you can join her,' said Thayer, extending his gun-arm so that the barrel of his 0.442-calibre Webley Bulldog was trained squarely on the top of Watson's bowed head. 'Absalon told me to fetch both of you, but he'll be just as happy with one.'

CHAPTER THIRTY-SEVEN

The Final Act

Holmes quickly stepped between them, saying: 'There's no need for that. Enough people have died already.' Gripping Watson by both arms, he helped him to stand up.

Watson said: 'But we just can't leave her here like this....'

'We won't,' Thayer said. He was an ugly, ungainly-looking man, with a sloping brow above dark, curiously emotionless eyes, a long hooked nose, thick lips and a bloodless, waxy skin. He stepped closer, quickly searched both men and put Watson's service revolver into his own jacket pocket. 'Now start walking.'

They headed deeper into the dark woods, the sound of fireworks and cheering fading with distance. The night was cooling rapidly. At length the trees thinned and a narrow, wheel-rutted path came into sight. The polished black coach with red wheel-spokes stood in the moonlight. A driver sat impassively on the high seat, his two-horse team standing patiently in the traces, steam billowing from their distended nostrils.

'Get inside,' Thayer told Holmes and Watson. As they obeyed, he turned to the driver. 'The girl killed Valentin and I killed the girl. I doubt if anyone will find the bodies right away, but you'll have to come back for them later.'

'D'accord,' said the driver.

Thayer climbed into the coach, his bulk weighing heavily on the thoroughbraces. Never taking his eyes off his prisoners, he sat across from them and then rapped on the carriage roof. 'Go!'

The driver cracked his whip and the coach raced off.

'Where are you taking us?' Watson asked Thayer.

'You'll find out when you get there.'

'I fancy our destination is somewhere in the Forêt Domaniale de Malvoisine,' Holmes remarked.

'You may "fancy" whatever you like,' Thayer said mockingly. 'It will not alter the final outcome.'

Watson glared at him. 'Whatever you have in mind, you won't get away with it,' he said. 'That I promise you.'

There was something so confident in his quiet threat that Thayer scowled and shifted uncomfortably. 'Shut your mouth!' he growled. 'Both of you.'

The drive took no more than an hour. At times the route meandered, but always they headed east through the darkness. At last Holmes spotted landmarks he had noted when he had followed Lydie from Paris and knew he had been right about their destination. The forest closed around them and the interior of the coach grew almost pitch-dark.

If they were going to make a move, it had to be now. And yet what chance did they stand in the confines of the carriage, with a man whose gun was aimed their way and ready to fire at the slightest squeeze of a finger? One of them might overpower him, but if it were at the expense of the other, the risk simply wasn't worth taking.

The trees thinned again. Holmes leaned forward and peered out of the window. A chateau lay beneath the moonlight, yellow light showing at some of its tall windows.

'And so we come to the final act in our drama,' he murmured.

'Final,' growled Thayer, 'for *you*.'

The carriage came to a halt before the stone steps and Thayer ordered them to get out. Another man was waiting on the steps. He also carried a gun. He was short and portly, with a jowly face and shaggy iron-grey hair that needed trimming – Absalon's right-hand man, Lacombe.

'Inside,' he told Holmes and Watson.

They entered the chateau, their footsteps echoing coldly across the flagstone floor. The lobby was brightly lit. After being so long in darkness the lamplight hurt their eyes. Men in dark suits either stood guard or hurried up or down the central cantilever staircase on some errand or other.

Alexandre Absalon was standing in the open double doorway of the study opposite the grand staircase. He looked as urbane as ever in a fashionable, tailored silver-grey suit. 'Gentlemen,' he said with a cruel smile. 'Please come inside.'

He sounded smugly pleased with himself.

Holmes and Watson followed him into the study, covered all the while by Thayer and Lacombe. Lacombe closed the doors behind them.

Absalon, now seated behind his desk, smiled mockingly at his visitors. 'Well, if it isn't the great Sherlock Holmes and his faithful companion, Docteur Watson,' he said. 'I hope you know that between you, you have caused the people I represent considerable inconvenience – and all, as it turns out, for naught.'

'François Fournier has withdrawn from your campaign,' Holmes said. 'I would not call that failure.'

Beside him, Watson started. So that's what Lydie had meant when she'd asked them if they'd heard the news.

'You have seen the late papers,' guessed Absalon.

'On the contrary,' Holmes said. 'We have been fully engaged at Versailles ever since this afternoon. However, it is the only logical conclusion I can draw. Before he died, your man Valentin told us you have no further interest in Verne.'

'We haven't. He is free to pick up the pieces of his life and go on his way ... provided he knows nothing that could possibly incriminate us. And that is why you are here, gentlemen. Before we dispose of you, you will tell us everything you know, or *think* you know, about our organization. You will also give us the names of everyone else who, thanks to you, even suspect that we exist.'

'At which time you will set about systematically murdering them all to protect your anonymity,' said Watson, his head-wound throbbing fiercely, 'beginning with Fournier, no doubt.'

'Fournier is safe enough,' Absalon said. 'He knows that should he ever speak out against us, we will make public his bisexuality.' Smiling, he added: 'He cannot ruin us without ruining himself.'

'Well, if you expect us to tell you anything other than that you and your organization are finished,' Watson said, 'you are in for a considerable disappointment.'

Absalon's smile broadened. His teeth were small and perfect. 'I admire your optimism, *Docteur*. But look how easily we broke Gaston Verne, with nothing more terrifying than the simple dripping of water. I fancy even you, M'sieur Holmes, will be willing to talk after we're through with you. But first we shall begin with you, *Docteur*. I do not believe that you share the same degree of courage as your companion. Nor do I think that he will stand by and watch you suffer for any length of time.'

Absalon suddenly lost his smile and his eyes turned deadly. 'Prepare the apparatus,' he told Lacombe.

Lacombe nodded and left the room. Absalon turned back to Holmes and Watson. 'It really is an ingenious contraption, gentlemen. One is strapped down in such a way that he can only watch as each single drop of ice-cold water is dripped slowly onto the centre of his forehead. Because the drops are administered at irregular intervals, the anticipation of each one builds until it becomes something ... exquisitely agonizing. Over time – less time than you may suppose – the victim realizes that, just as water can eventually wear a hole in even the hardest and most seemingly resilient slab of stone, so too can it work this same effect upon human flesh and bone.

With each single drop he begins to picture the irreversible damage being done to his skull, the pressure of the bone pressing down upon his brain, the destruction of cell and nerve and tissue. It really is an inspired form of torture. So simple, yet so effective—'

Before he could say more, there came a sudden, harsh jangling from the front of the house that sounded unsettlingly like an alarm bell, followed rapidly by a series of indistinct but undeniably urgent yells. For the briefest moment Absalon looked alarmed.

An instant later the double doors burst open and Lacombe lumbered back in, his expression one of panic.

'What is it?' snapped Absalon.

'They're coming, sir! Godenot was just turning the carriage around when he saw them marching up the lane!'

'Saw whom?'

'The army, sir.'

'*Army?*'

'*Oui, m'sieur.*'

Absalon went white. 'You idiot! You must be mistaken—'

'He isn't,' snarled Watson. 'It *is* the army.' And to Thayer: 'Remember, I promised you you'd never get away with this.'

All at once something finally made sense to Holmes. He looked at Watson and said softly: 'Gillet. *That's* where you went on Wednesday! You went to see Henri Gillet!'

'Exactly,' said Watson. 'And after I finished telling him everything we had uncovered, he used the authority invested in him by the *Ministère de la Justice* and mobilized the army, with orders to watch and wait and seize the first chance we gave them to destroy the Knaves once and for all!'

———— ℮ ℈ ————

'Light the Fuses!'

Absalon motioned to Lacombe and Thayer to keep Holmes and Watson covered, then hurried to the window. Pulling aside the curtains, he looked out.

What he saw chilled his blood. For there, quick-marching up the lane in a long column of twos was indeed the army. Led by mounted officers, the soldiers wore iron-blue greatcoats and *kepis*, bright red trousers tucked into their boots and carried Lebel rifles with long cruciform bayonets attached. It was a grimly inspiring sight, and one that shook Absalon's confidence.

'What are we going to do, sir?' Lacombe said fearfully.

Turning from the window, Absalon hid his own fear behind a disdainful smile. 'Do?' he sneered. 'Why, fight them, of course!'

'But, sir, they outnumber us ten to—'

'Hold your tongue, you fool!' He paused as outside the approaching soldiers began shouting: '*Pour la France! Pour la France!*'

'It seems,' Holmes said drily, 'you have stirred up quite a hornets' nest.'

Absalon started to reply, but before he could do so a commanding voice cried out: '*Attention, inside the house! I call upon you to surrender in the name of the French government!*'

Absalon stood there, glaring, teeth gritted. There was a long moment of absolute silence, then the same voice shouted:

'*I repeat. This is the French government! I call upon you to surrender! You are surrounded and we will use force if necessary!*'

'Sir ...' began Lacombe.

Absalon struck him across the face, silencing him. 'There will be no surrender,' he snarled, adding: 'Tell the men to stand fast and hold them back as long as possible!'

Then, as Lacombe remained there, unwilling to leave: 'Tell them, damn you!'

For another moment Lacombe defiantly stood there. Then as Thayer aimed his pistol at him, Lacombe grudgingly left.

'A lot of people will die if you don't give this up,' Watson warned.

Absalon snorted disdainfully. 'Do you actually think that would trouble me, *Docteur?*'

Before Watson could reply they heard the sudden rattle of gunfire outside the front of the house, mingled with the shattering of windows and the yells of men in combat. Absalon returned to the window and peered out.

Outside, soldiers were advancing *en masse* across the lawn, firing as they came. Their bayonets glinted in the moonlight. From their positions around the house Absalon's men fired back at the onrushing troopers, killing or incapacitating several in the front line. But all around them the others still pressed forward. Nothing could stop the charge.

Absalon, sensing he was finished, turned from the window and started to give Thayer an order. He stopped as the door burst open and Lacombe rushed back in, exclaiming: 'They're storming the house, sir! I'm not sure how long we can hold them back.'

'Surrender,' urged Holmes.

Absalon ignored him. 'Light the fuses,' he told Lacombe.

'But, sir—!'

'Do it, damn you!'

As Lacombe hurried from the study, Absalon glared at his

prisoners. 'You may have won the battle, gentlemen, but you will not win the war.'

'Surely you're not going to blow up the chateau?' Holmes said.

Absalon gathered some papers from his desk and stuffed them into his jacket pockets. 'We have prepared for every eventuality, including this one,' he said. 'The cellar holds a number of plain wooden boxes, each of which contains sawdust soaked in glyceryl trinitrate. To each box is connected a detonator cap and a fuse, each fuse carefully timed to allow us precisely fifteen minutes to make good our escape. Yes,' he concluded. 'I am going to blow up the chateau.'

'Just to protect the contents of that safe?' said Holmes, indicating the heavy brown-and-black Chubb in the corner.

Absalon smiled coolly. 'We are nothing if not thorough, M'sieur Holmes. If we're forced to set up again elsewhere, we will not leave even the tiniest scrap of evidence behind us.' He turned to Thayer. 'Kill them, and then meet me outside by the bridge.'

It was then that Watson made his move. With nothing to lose, he lowered his shoulder and charged Thayer, driving him back into a stool. Thayer went sprawling. Watson leapt on him, all too aware that this was the man who had killed Lydie; and even as Thayer tried to bring his revolver up Watson slammed him unmercifully on the jaw.

Absalon, seeing what was happening, quickly opened one of the desk drawers and grabbed the gun lying inside. But Holmes had already launched himself across the desk. He tackled Absalon, his momentum landing both of them in a heap by the wall.

Thayer, meanwhile, shoved Watson aside and again tried to raise his revolver. Watson grabbed the stool and threw it at him. Then as Thayer rolled aside to avoid the makeshift missile, Watson snatched an unlit lamp off the table and hurled it at him.

Thayer batted the lamp away. Its funnel shattered, showering him with broken glass and kerosene. Before he could recover, Watson was on him. He grasped Thayer's right wrist and bent it backwards. Thayer cried out and dropped his gun. As Watson reached for it, Thayer kneed him in the face.

Watson staggered backwards into some furniture and went down hard. His head struck the floor, momentarily stunning him. Stars blinded him. When his vision cleared he heard Holmes shout his name.

His head snapped up just as Thayer pulled Watson's own service revolver from his pocket.

Watson quickly aimed Thayer's pistol at him and squeezed the trigger.

The impact of the bullet doubled Thayer over, blood spreading from a wound in the centre of his chest. His eyes widened, blood ran from his slack mouth and he fell back, dead before he hit the floor.

CHAPTER THIRTY-NINE

Poetic Justice

Outside, the sounds of combat were now closer and more violent. Gunfire filled the night. Hand-to-hand combat began. Steel clashed against steel. Cries of pain came from the dying and the wounded. Corpses littered the lawn. Their comrades leaped over them and continued their attack.

The soldiers' relentless firing took heavy toll of Absalon's men. Their bodies hung limply from windows or were slumped down in doorways, blood puddling around them.

'Pour la France! Pour la France!'

Bullets shattered the study window. Flying glass rained onto the hardwood floor. Alarmed, everyone shrank back.

'Give up!' Holmes told Absalon. 'While there's still time.'

'Never!' grated Absalon.

Suddenly they heard wood splintering as the front door was breached. There followed a confusion of gunshots, then silence and then calls from the officers, demanding surrender. A few scattered shots followed, but after that all shooting ceased.

Watson shouted: *'Gillet! In here!'*

Moments later the double doors burst open and Lacombe stumbled in, propelled by Henri Gillet. A short, stocky man of forty with curly grey hair and merry blue eyes, Gillet gave Lacombe another push and then he looked about him. His gaze settled first on Watson, then on the body of Thayer, then Holmes, and finally Alexandre Absalon.

'*Bonsoir,* M'sieur Holmes,' he said, bowing. 'My wife and I are still awaiting the pleasure of your company.'

Animated voices were heard outside the study. Moments later Michel, Mathes and two officers hurried in.

'Search the house!' Gillet ordered.

'No!' snapped Holmes. 'Wait!'

'What is it?' Gillet demanded.

Holmes turned to Lacombe. 'Did you light the fuses?'

Lacombe nodded and stared fearfully at Absalon.

'The cellar is full of explosives,' Watson told Gillet. 'We only have a few minutes to evacuate the building.'

Gillet confronted Lacombe. 'Is there still time to put these fuses out?'

'P-Perhaps – if we do it now,' said Lacombe. 'But it will be very close, *m'sieur.*'

Holmes said: 'Then let them burn.' To Gillet he added: 'Get your men and your prisoners to safety.'

'What about you?'

'M'sieur Absalon and I are going to stay here.'

Absalon looked alarmed. '*What?*'

'I have reason to believe that whatever is in that safe is vital to the continuation of the Knaves,' Holmes said. He paused and looked at Watson before continuing: 'A fine, brave lady of our acquaintance tried to tell us as much before this man Thayer killed her earlier this evening. Now, we do not have the time to move the safe, nor can we spare the time to work out the combination by ourselves. For that we need *you,* Absalon. And if you refuse to cooperate, then the explosion will destroy you as certainly as it will destroy the evidence you hope to keep from us.'

'You're mad!' Absalon said.

'Let us see, shall we?' said Holmes. 'The rest of you – leave now, while you have the chance.'

Gillet, realizing Holmes was right, pushed Lacombe towards the door. '*Allez! Allez!* Everyone out of here – now!'

Holmes waited for Gillet and his men to leave and then said to Watson: 'You too, old friend.'

Watson shook his head and retrieved his service revolver from Thayer. 'If it's all the same to you,' he said, 'I'll stay.'

'So will I,' added Michel.

'You're all insane,' said Inspector Mathes. 'But God help me, I'll never forgive myself if I don't stay and see it through with you.'

Absalon looked at them. 'You fools! I have spent the last ten years serving the Knaves, watching the organization grow and spread and slowly but surely gain influence and power! Do you really think I would betray all that just to save my own skin?'

Holmes sat on the edge of the desk and folded his arms. 'We shall see,' he said calmly.

Watson took out his pocket watch and checked the time. 'I estimate that we have perhaps eight minutes left.'

Absalon sneered. 'Eight minutes, eight seconds – I will never betray my cause.'

Michel flopped into a chair. 'Then it will be my pleasure to watch you die, *m'sieur.* You, who caused my parents so much ugliness.'

Mathes nodded. 'I agree. To think that your organization has infiltrated and corrupted the force I hold so dear ... *oui,* it will be a pleasure to watch as you begin your journey to hell.'

'Seven minutes,' said Watson.

'You're bluffing,' Absalon scoffed. 'You're all bluffing.'

'Do we look as if we are bluffing?' asked Holmes.

'Six minutes.'

Watson kept his voice as level as he could, but he began to wonder if Holmes had underestimated his opponent. For a moment it was on the tip of his tongue to say that perhaps they should cut their losses and leave while they still could. After all, where was the sense in four decent men losing their lives for the sake of an evil fifth?

But then he remembered Lydie's last words: *The safe ...*

Absalon clearly kept something there that could help them bring about the destruction of the Knaves. So, calmly, he announced: 'Five minutes.'

'All right!' said Absalon. 'You win! I will give you the combination – but in return I demand immunity from prosecution.'

'Agreed,' Holmes said immediately.

'*M'sieur,*' Mathes protested, 'it is not for you to accede to such a demand. You have no authority—'

'You have my word upon it,' Holmes told Absalon.

'Four minutes,' said Watson. 'Hurry, man!'

Absalon went to the safe, knelt and began turning the dial first one way, then the other. Watson shifted his gaze from Absalon's busy fingers to the second hand as it swept around the face of his pocket watch. It was imagination, surely, but it seemed to him that the seconds were ticking away alarmingly fast.

Absalon twisted the brass handle and opened the safe's two doors. 'There,' he said dejectedly.

Holmes said, 'Here, take these,' and began to remove stacks of documents and folders. He gave the first pile to Michel, the second to Mathes, a third to Watson. Then keeping the last batch himself, he, Watson and the others raced from the room.

As they ran, Watson thought: *We had only four minutes. Surely they must be up now?*

The lobby was littered with broken glass and dead bodies. Footsteps clattering over the flagstones, they reached the front door. Michel jerked it open. As he did he dropped several folders and wasted valuable seconds as he fumbled around trying to scoop them up. Holmes stopped to help, 'Quickly, my friend! Quickly, now!' and then the two of them rushed after the others.

Finally, they were all outside. They paused by the front steps, gulping in the cold night air as they looked around for Gillet, the soldiers and their prisoners.

'*Over here!*' Gillet waved to them from behind a low stone wall bordering the grass in front of the tree-line.

The five men sprinted for the wall, Holmes bringing up the rear. From here he was able to keep an eye on Absalon and at the same time be sure that Watson kept up with them on his game leg.

The group were about halfway to the wall when, behind them, the chateau exploded.

Momentarily, the night became bright as day. Still they ran, their fleeing shadows stretching long and misshapen before them. Burning debris flew everywhere. There followed a racketing blast of sound that sent a shockwave through them. An unstoppable wave of heat punched them in the back and sent them sprawling. Everyone lay where they fell, curling themselves into protective balls, arms covering their heads, waiting to see if there would be any more explosions.

They did not have to wait long.

Seconds later there was another deafening explosion, then another and another, each lighting up the darkness until – suddenly there was a roaring, ripping, tearing, whistling sound of ancient stone being torn apart and flung in every direction.

'*Run!*' yelled Holmes, scrambling to his feet. 'Save yourselves!'

Everyone jumped up and, still clutching the files and documents they had risked their lives for, raced towards the wall.

Behind them huge concrete blocks came smashing back to earth, along with splintered, burning rafters and the razor-edged remnants of roof tiles, flagstones and glass. They slammed into the ground, bouncing and rolling after Holmes, Watson and the others like pursing demons.

Incredibly, all five men managed to stay a step ahead of the raining debris.

Behind the wall Gillet and the troops yelled encouragement as they waved them on.

It was close, but they made it. As one they scrambled over the wall and ducked down behind its protection. Moments later tumbling, flaming debris slammed against the wall. It shuddered and in some places cracked, but remained standing.

It was some time before Holmes and Watson dared put their heads above the parapet. All that remained of the chateau was a jumbled, ragged, blazing pile of rubble.

Once everyone's safety was assured, Gillet ordered his officers to have the troops put out the fire. He then joined Holmes, Watson and the others, who stood nearby. Though unharmed, all were covered in dirt and trying to cough the smoke and dust from their lungs.

'I hope the risk was worth it,' said Gillet.

'I have no doubt that it was,' said Holmes. He indicated the evidence piled on the ground. 'Just as I am equally certain that the contents of these files will prove to be most ... illuminating.'

'And remember,' said Absalon, his once-immaculate clothes now torn and filthy, 'I have been promised immunity from prosecution for cooperating.'

'Upon whose authority?' demanded Gillet.

'Upon mine,' Holmes said. 'I felt it was a promise you would gladly honour, Henri ... given that I could make no such assurance on behalf of the Knaves.'

Absalon paled. 'W-what was that?'

Holmes eyed him bleakly. 'The evidence you have supplied, M'sieur Absalon, will doubtless enable the French government to bring about the demise of the group you held so dear. But that will take time. And until the last of the Knaves has been rooted out, I am confident that you will be high upon their list for retribution.'

Absalon sagged. 'No!' he whispered. 'No, you can't do that!'

'It is out of my hands,' Holmes said with great satisfaction. 'Once it becomes clear how you betrayed them, your compatriots will be out for blood. No matter where you go or where you hide or how completely you try to disguise your true identity, they will find you and make sure you pay for your treachery.'

In light of the crackling flames his smile was humourless. 'It may be tomorrow, or the next day, or the day after that. But rest assured, M'sieur Absalon, it *will* happen. And sooner rather than later. One morning when Watson and I are back in London, I will pick up *The Times* and with much delight will read that you have become another victim of the organization you once prized so much. In other words, my dear M'sieur Absalon, you have just become a marked man, just as you yourself marked Gaston Verne, Jules Verne, Gabriel Bessette and Lydie Denier for death.'

'Poetic justice,' muttered Watson. 'It's not a very pleasant feeling, is it?'

Epilogue

It was a bright afternoon, and for late March the weather was pleasantly warm. Tables had been set up overlooking the manicured grounds behind Verne's house in Amiens. Here, shaded by colourful umbrellas, the writer's guests looked on, amused, as on hands and knees he played with the grandson he had seldom seen while estranged from his son.

At last Verne sat back, breathless with activity and laughter. The year-old toddler, who was named after Michel, quickly crawled to his grandfather and stared up at him, eyes alive with merriment.

'Enough!' Verne pleaded. 'I am an old man now ... far too old to keep up with a young sprout like you!'

But the boy would hear none of it. He tugged on Verne's sleeve and giggled, anxious to continue the game.

'Well ... at least let me ... get my breath back ... first,' managed Verne.

At one of the tables, Honorine chatted with her pregnant daughter-in-law, Jeanne. She was eager to get to know the attractive girl, whom everyone called 'Maja', and Maja in turn was eager to know her. At nineteen the former Jeanne Raboul was much younger than her husband, but deeply devoted to him. One could see that in the loving way she gazed at him, as he stood nearby enjoying the sight of his father bonding with his grandchild.

At another table Watson watched the Verne family finally getting along and beamed at Holmes beside him. 'Isn't it wonderful to see them so happy?' he remarked.

'It is indeed.'

'And just think, we were at least partly responsible for it.'

'Modesty, thy name is John Watson,' Holmes said. But he was joking. And raising his lemonade glass to Watson, he added: 'May I propose a toast, old friend?'

'Please do.'

'To the memory of Lydie Denier.'

Immediately Watson felt his throat tighten. 'I hope you mean that,' he said, touching glasses.

'My dear man, when have you ever heard me speak of death in jest?'

Watson smiled, satisfied. 'Thank you, Holmes. That means a great deal to me.'

They both drank.

'Regardless of her motives,' Holmes continued, 'she decided to help us bring about the destruction of the Knaves, and albeit indirectly, she did exactly that by communicating to us the importance of the contents of Absalon's safe.'

That was, of course, an understatement. Once Henri Gillet and the *Ministère de la Justice* had had the opportunity to examine the contents of the safe, it became clear that they had more than enough evidence to bring about a series of arrests at just about every level of society. All across France, businessmen, politicians, judges – even Edouard Orand, the director of the Sanatorium de Russy, and the man named Prideaux, who had killed Gabriel Bessette in his Amiens jail cell – had been arrested and were awaiting trial.

The files and folders had contained the names, addresses and aliases of its many members, details of the banks in which the Knaves' funds were held, a detailed list of payments – *bribes* – as well as the names of the recipients. It was enough to keep Gillet busy for a long time, and to make him a very happy man in the process.

'To Lydie,' murmured Watson, sadly.

'And to you, old friend,' said Holmes, smiling. 'Remember, it was your concern for my welfare that brought us to France, and your decision to enlist Henri's help. Let us make no bones about it – without your initiative and his intervention, we would have been finished. That, I believe, makes it *twice* you have saved my life in the past few weeks.'

'I wouldn't go as far as to say that,' Watson said self-consciously.

'Please, no false modesty,' Holmes chided. 'It rankles me as much as bragging.'

'Very well,' Watson said, secretly pleased. 'I shall accept my role in this escapade with as much dignity and aplomb as I can muster.'

Holmes wasn't listening. 'Though in the end,' he admitted, 'despite the fact that your idea of a rest cure brought with it no shortage of mortal danger, I have to tell you that I have seldom felt as invigorated as I do today.'

'Careful, Holmes. That sounds awfully like a compliment.'

'It was meant to be. You are a very wise man, Watson … for I cannot remember when I last enjoyed a holiday quite so much!'

'Tell that to your bees,' Watson joked. 'I'm sure it would relieve the monotony of their hum-drum lives.'

'Never knock monotony,' Holmes said with a rare smile. 'For from monotony comes the pure, sweet honey you so enjoy.'

Authors' Note

It hardly needs saying that *Sherlock Holmes and the Knave of Hearts* is a work of fiction. But it is fiction based – at least in part – upon fact.

As reported in all the major newspapers of the time, Gaston Verne did indeed make an attempt upon his uncle's life on 9 March 1886. Gaston was known to be mentally unstable, and records indicate that in the months leading up to the shooting he had been under medical observation for his strange behaviour and acute paranoia. Many historians believe this 'observation' took place in an asylum in Blois, where he had been committed by his father, Paul Verne. However, it is highly unlikely that the true facts of the matter will ever be known.

Immediately after the shooting, the Vernes embarked upon a campaign of what, today, we would call 'damage limitation'. They offered any number of spurious 'motives' for Gaston's actions, none of them even coming close to the truth, and many of them frankly ludicrous. The Vernes gave no interviews and pressed no charges. And Gaston himself was packed off to a psychiatric clinic in Luxembourg, where he died sometime around 1916, at the age of 56.

However, it is beyond dispute that Gaston travelled by train to Amiens on that fateful day in the March of '86, and the subsequent shooting did happen very much as it is presented here. Gaston's first shot missed. The second smashed into Jules Verne's left shin. A botched operation made the removal of the bullet impossible, and Verne limped for the rest of his life.

Gaston offered no resistance during his arrest. Nor did he ever explain why he shot his favourite uncle, except to blame 'family affairs of such sensitivity that I am unable to divulge them'.

Some sources speculate that Gaston was not actually Verne's nephew at all, but rather his son; the illegitimate progeny of a liaison with Paul Verne's wife Berthe. But many more rumours abound that he had been Verne's lover, and decided to shoot him after discovering that his uncle had found himself a new beau. The one word Gaston uttered during the murder attempt, *'Salaud!'* or 'Bastard!', offers no real clues.

Still, the possibility that Jules and Gaston Verne indulged in a homosexual affair isn't as far-fetched as it might at first appear. The truth of Verne's sexuality has long been the source of great debate. He did indeed enjoy the company of younger men. In particular, his long and intimate friendship with Aristide Briand, who was some thirty years his junior, helped to inspire our story. Briand served no less than eleven terms as prime minister of France between 1909 and 1929.